HEMLOCK HOUSE

Also by KATIE COTUGNO

KATIE COTUGNO

HEMLOCK HOUSE

A LIAR'S BEACH NOVEL

DELACORTE PRESS

alloyentertainment

Text copyright © 2024 by Katie Cotugno and Alloy Entertainment
Jacket photograph copyright © 2024 by Iappes/iStock

All rights reserved. Published in the United States by Delacorte Press, an imprint of Random House Children's Books, a division of Penguin Random House LLC, New York.

Delacorte Press is a registered trademark and the colophon is a trademark of Penguin Random House LLC.

GetUnderlined.com

Educators and librarians, for a variety of teaching tools, visit us at RHTeachersLibrarians.com

Library of Congress Cataloging-in-Publication Data is available upon request.
ISBN 978-0-593-43332-4 (hardcover) — ISBN 978-0-593-43333-1 (lib. bdg.) —
ISBN 978-0-593-43334-8 (ebook) — ISBN 978-0-593-89758-4 (int'l edition)

The text of this book is set in 11.25-point Adobe Garamond Pro.
Interior design by Cathy Bobak

Printed in the United States of America
10 9 8 7 6 5 4 3 2 1
First Edition

For Shana, Erin, and Adrienne. They know why.

1

Thursday, 10/17/24

A FACT THAT SEEMS RELEVANT TO MENTION BEFORE
we begin, though of course it didn't occur to me to look it up
until much later: statistically, it's actually very unlikely for a person to fall victim to a violent crime in the city of Cambridge,
Massachusetts.

The rate of robbery is remarkably low, at just 52.6 annually
per 100,000 residents, compared to 135.5 throughout the United
States and 118 just across the Charles River in Boston. Rates of
assault are admittedly higher, though occurrences still clock in
well below the national average, with a rate of 224.3 per 100,000
residents.

And murder? Well, murder is rarest of all, with a rate of just
0.8 per 100,000 residents, compared to a national average of 6.1.
"Even if you were *trying* to get murdered in Cambridge," Holiday
mused later, eyes narrowed behind the metal rims of her giant
glasses, "you'd really have to, like, apply yourself."

At least, that's what we'd always thought.

Anyway, like I said, I didn't know any of that the fall of my first year at Harvard, and I probably wouldn't have cared about it even if I did. Anyone trying to tell me would have had to shout over the sound of my teammates egging me on as I stood on a metal folding chair and shotgunned a hard seltzer in the dining room of the lax house, the sweet, fizzy dregs of it trickling down the side of my neck and into the collar of my hoodie.

"He's got style, he's got grace!" Cam declared as I finished, clapping me hard between my shoulder blades. Every first-year lacrosse player was paired with an upperclassman mentor, and he was mine; in the weeks since I'd arrived on campus he'd not only set my daily workout plan and invited me over to watch the Pats on Sundays but had also imparted such valuable information as which dining halls had the best cereal selection and never to use the shower stall next to Ryan Jakes, a junior defenseman who was notorious for pissing into the communal drain. "He's Miss United States."

"Thank you, thank you." I wiped my mouth with the back of my hand, fully aware that this was absolutely not, under any circumstances, an achievement for which to feel proud of myself, but feeling a tiny bit proud of myself anyway. It's always kind of a high-wire act, trying to figure out where and how to fit in on a new team. If *cheerful drunk* wasn't quite what I wanted to be known as over the next four years, it was a better position to start from than *whiny little bitch who can't hang.* "As always, I appreciate your love and support."

"Let's see him go again," suggested Dex Rutland, a sophomore midfielder. The grin on his pale, freckled face just missed being friendly. "What do you say, Linden?"

Cam looked at me, the question clear in the wrinkle of his smooth brown forehead. I was just about to oblige—one thing about me, for better or for worse, is that I will basically never back down from a dare—when I felt a slice of cold air from the direction of the foyer and caught sight of a familiar cardinal-red peacoat slipping in through the front door.

"Hey!" I called a beat too quickly, hopping down off the chair so fast my bad ankle nearly gave out and left me sprawled on the dingy Persian rug. I ignored the goading jeers of my teammates as I threaded my eager way through the crowd. "You came."

"I came," Greer agreed with a forbearing smile, tucking her hands into her pockets and popping up onto the toes of her boots, pressing her cold cheek against mine. She wore a pair of round tortoiseshell glasses and an oversized L.L.Bean pullover, a vintage Tiffany bean around her neck. "I like old things," she'd told me once, the two of us sprawled on my bed back at the Western Massachusetts boarding school we'd attended together. Now, two years later, I couldn't help but hope that included boyfriends. "Hi."

"Hi yourself," I said, my heart vibrating dorkily in my chest. "I didn't think you were going to show."

"I almost didn't," she confessed, "but Bri is already here somewhere, so I figured—" She broke off, eyes narrowing as she looked across the warm, crowded living room, where Dex had graciously taken over in my stead and was already halfway through a twenty-four-ounce can of White Claw. "I thought you said this was going to be, like, a chill, low-key kind of thing."

"Is this not low-key?" I asked sheepishly, my voice getting lost as the rest of the guys erupted into cheers over my shoulder. Most of the upperclassmen on the lacrosse team had moved off campus a few years back, when Harvard randomized their housing selection process and made it harder for teams to self-sort into particular dorms. Since then, the lease on this place had been passed from one lax captain to the next, the walls and floors and carpets bearing the not-inconsiderable scars of hundreds of parties way wilder than this one. "Come on," I shouted over the noise, jerking my thumb in the direction of the kitchen. "I'll get you a drink."

Greer let me take her hand as we weaved through the crush of bodies in the narrow center hallway, past the once-grand front staircase that led up to the bedrooms and the tiny little telephone nook tucked underneath. "That's cute," she said when she noticed it, and she sounded sincere, which I took to mean she hadn't looked closely enough to see the giant, erupting cock and balls carved into the woodwork of the antique bench.

The kitchen was mercifully empty, the heavy door swinging shut behind us and muffling the clatter of the party. Greer hopped up onto the scarred Formica counter as I pulled a beer from one of the picnic coolers lined up beside the door to the cluttered mudroom, handing it over before grabbing one for myself and perching against the edge of the wobbly wooden table. "So," I said, reaching out and clinking my can against hers, "what's up?"

Greer shook her head, smirking a little at the question. "Not too much," she said, the heels of her boots banging lightly against the worn lower cabinets. The kitchen at the lax house was huge, with two stainless steel fridges parked side by side and a massive industrial range that always looked a little grimy; the sink was a big old double-basin situation with separate taps for hot water and cold. "How about you?"

"Oh, you know." I shrugged, the silence stretching out between us for a few seconds too long not to be awkward. I took a big gulp of my beer. I'd forgotten this, how back before Greer and I started dating my junior year at Bartley I was perpetually tongue-tied around her. How I could never think of the right thing to say. "Not too much . . . either."

Jesus Christ. What was wrong with me? I was generally pretty good with girls—women? I guessed they were technically women, now that we were in college—though you'd never have known it by the way my mind was suddenly blanker than an old-fashioned Scantron sheet at the beginning of exam week. "Okay, can we—" I started, just as Greer said, "Look, Linden—"

Both of us broke off, smiling a little wanly. "Go for it," she told me, at the same time that I shook my head: "Sorry, what were you—?"

Another long moment of silence. I was just about to excuse myself to go drown politely in the Quabbin Reservoir when all at once Greer's roommate, Bri, spilled through the door of the kitchen, a human tornado made of charm bracelets and expensive perfume.

"You *are* here!" she accused, throwing her arms around Greer like they'd last seen each other on the battlefields of Antietam and not, presumably, a couple of hours before in their suite back at Hemlock, one of the nine upperclassmen houses nestled between the Square and the river. Bri's hair was the same dark chestnut as Greer's, though she was taller, with the slightly muscley shoulders of a girl who had played field hockey in high school but now mostly did the elliptical machine at the gym. She was wearing a pair of open-toed shoes with heels so high I wondered briefly how she'd managed to walk all the way here without smashing her skull open like a melon on the crooked, brick-lined sidewalks. Also, she was visibly shit-faced. "Somebody said they'd seen you come in and I was like, *No, there's no way she's here and did not find me immediately,* though I see now"—here Bri flicked me in the side with one polished fingernail before making a beeline for the cluster of sticky, half-empty alcohol bottles on the counter opposite Greer—"that you were busy rekindling your tortured high school romance."

"*Bri,*" Greer chided, her cheeks reddening even as she rolled her eyes. "For fuck's sake."

I took another sip of my beer, feeling my own face warm at the merciless baldness of Bri's assessment. I'd known Greer was at Harvard when I got recruited, obviously—she was a sophomore now, studying to become a spinal surgeon just like both of her parents—but we hadn't run into each other until three weeks into the semester, when I'd rounded a corner at the Coop and there she was, considering the ball caps, backpack slung over one shoulder and her hair in a shiny French braid. "It's you," she said, like she didn't quite believe it.

"I'm not stalking you," I blurted immediately, flustered even though there was a part of me that had been waiting for this exact encounter since the moment I stepped onto campus. We'd only talked once since we'd broken up at the spring of my junior year at Bartley: two summers ago she'd called me to report that her parents' insurance company was going to want to talk to me about what had happened the night of the car accident that had both shattered my ankle and effectively ended our relationship, and she'd appreciate it if I stuck to our story. "I mean, I guess that's also what I would say if I was stalking you? But. I'm not."

"Okay . . . ," she said slowly, the corners of her lips quirking just a little. "I didn't think you were."

"I go here now," I told her, my voice weirdly loud in the quiet bookstore. My hands felt too big, a pair of old phone books attached to the ends of my arms. "I'm playing lacrosse."

Greer nodded. "Yeah," she said, "I heard something about that. I'm glad it worked out." She smiled for real this time, like the sun coming up over the Charles in the morning. "Hi, Linden."

I exhaled, my shoulders dropping back down to where they belonged. It was useless to pretend I didn't still think about her. It was useless to pretend I didn't still care. "Hi, Greer."

In the weeks since then we'd hung out a few times, meeting for coffee at the hipster place in the Smith Center and going to a free concert on the Esplanade. Every single time, I shoved a piece of gum in my mouth just in case, but so far we seemed to be stuck decisively in neutral. Which was fine, obviously—it wasn't like I thought Greer owed me a hookup for nostalgia's sake or whatever. I just . . . still liked her, that was all. I was pretty sure that neither one of us could quite decide if she still liked me back.

Now Bri ignored our visible discomfort, plucking a half-empty bottle from the makeshift bar and waggling it in Greer's direction. "Want me to make you one of these?" she asked.

Greer tilted her head, her expression equal parts curious and fond. "Just to clarify: by *one of these,* you mean a generous glug of Fireball in a red plastic cup?"

"Exactly." Bri's smile was dazzling. "Craft cocktail, baby." She poured for a three count, splashing some cinnamon-flavored whiskey onto the counter and wiping it up with her bare hand before heading for the living room. Then, on second thought, she doubled back and took the bottle, too. "You guys be good."

"We always are," Greer promised. She waited until Bri was gone, then shook her head at me. "Sorry. That girl is my best friend at college, but she is a hot mess."

"Is it an act?" I asked, taking a chance and boosting myself up onto the counter next to her, the sides of our pinkies just brushing. "Like, a fun party girl thing?"

"I mean, yes and no?" Greer shrugged. "Don't get me wrong, she's a literal genius, all her professors love her, but she also is very much getting obliterated five nights out of the week."

"That's a lot of nights."

"It is, in fact, five-sevenths of the nights," Greer agreed. "She's also now putting her Adderall up her nose instead of just like, taking it the normal way like everybody else, which feels sort of alarming to me? But she's on the dean's list and I'm barely clinging to my sanity, so what the fuck do I know. I should probably just try it her way."

I smiled, bumping her arm lightly with mine. "You know some things," I said.

That made her laugh. "Thank you," she said, dropping her

head briefly onto my shoulder. "I do. I know like, one or two things."

"Three things at least," I continued.

"Well, don't overdo it," Greer said, holding a hand up. "You're going to make me blush."

"It *is* wild here, though," I admitted quietly. "At this school, I mean." The truth was, I still couldn't quite believe I'd gotten in: the accident had left my ankle smashed to powder, with any chance at a lacrosse scholarship—not to mention my entire future—hanging precariously in the balance. It wasn't lost on me how lucky I was to be at this party right now and not bagging groceries at Market Basket half a mile away. "I know that like, the first rule of being at Harvard is to act like being at Harvard is no big deal and that you always knew you were smart and accomplished enough to deserve it and the work doesn't make you want to lie down in a ditch? But I'll tell you, Greer: sometimes the work makes me want to lie down in a ditch."

"Same, obviously." She took a sip of her beer. "Do you wish you were somewhere else?"

I shook my head. "I do not."

"Me either." Greer smiled. "I know it's so dorky, but you know what my family is like. Every single one of them went here. They literally put me in a Harvard onesie to bring me home from the hospital after I was born." She ran her thumb over the mouth of the bottle. "Can I tell you something so fucking corny?"

"Cornier than the Harvard onesie?" I teased.

"Impressively, yes." Greer wrinkled her nose. "It was so nice and fallish outside this afternoon that I put that old Cranberries song on my headphones and just, like, walked back and forth across campus a couple of times pretending I was in a movie."

I burst out laughing, I couldn't help it. "Oh yeah, that is really fucking corny."

"Fuck you!" Greer punched me in the arm. "You like it."

"I do," I admitted, ducking my head a little closer. "I . . . yeah. I mean. You know I do."

I was just about to ask her if she wanted to get out of here and head back to her suite when the kitchen door swung abruptly open and Hunter Hayes strolled through in a hoodie and a backward Whalers cap: "There you are," he said when he spotted me. "I've been looking."

"Well." I winced. "Here I am." Hunter was a senior forward, cocaptain of the lax team. Every time I looked at him I saw his entire future laid out before me like the battered game of Chutes and Ladders that lived in our entertainment unit when I was a kid: business school at Wharton, followed by a stint at an investment bank in Boston and a successful congressional run in the small Maine district where his dad was a wealthy real estate attorney. Two years after that, a scandal involving the nanny, his blond wife smiling tightly beside him as he stood at a podium and recommitted himself to family values.

"So I see," he agreed now, baring his teeth at me. "Need you to go on a beer run."

"Wait." I frowned: if there was anything we had more than enough of at this party, it was alcohol. I could see at least half a dozen twelve-packs of cans from where I was sitting, not to mention the scrum of bottles on the counter. "Seriously?"

"Seriously," Hunter said cheerfully. "Always be prepared, am I right?" His gaze cut to Greer, his gaze sharpening just the slightest bit. "Unless, of course, you're otherwise engaged."

Greer made a face. I didn't, but only because I didn't want to take a cuff directly to the side of my head. I was used to this: it was the same for all the first-year lax players, the knowledge that you could be called upon at any moment to drop everything you were doing to run some inane, vaguely humiliating errand for an upperclassman—dropping off laundry, picking up foot cream at CVS. George Patel, another first-year, had spent the entirety of last weekend picking all the yellow Skittles out of an enormous bag from Costco because one of the senior defensemen swore they made his pee smell weird. It wasn't anything out of the ordinary, really. I'd been playing private-school sports since I was fourteen; I could take a little bit of hazing. In fact, there was a part of me that even welcomed the chance to show the rest of the team that I wasn't about to crack under pressure. *Look how stoically this guy scrubs toilets,* I imagined them saying. *Linden's no whiny little flea, no sir.*

Still, I couldn't help but feel like something about it was different with Hunter—that he'd singled me out for a special kind of torture, like there was something about me specifically that had rubbed him the wrong way from the moment I'd stepped onto campus. He'd pissed in my cleats once, back in September. The previous Saturday he'd made me eat six Tasty Burgers in a row while he watched.

Also, not for nothing, I didn't love the way he was looking at Greer.

"Okay," I said now, glancing in her direction, trying to gauge whether or not she was disappointed at the prospect of my leaving. "I'm going. Any kind of beer in particular?"

"You can use your judgment," Hunter said generously. "Nothing cheap, though. We're gentlemen around here, are we not?" He smiled again, his canines sharp and gleaming. "Greer, sweetheart. Good to see you."

"Hunter." She rolled her eyes indulgently. "Always a pleasure."

"It is, right?" He reached out and squeezed her knee through her jeans, quick and casual. "I think so too."

"I hate that dude," I said once he was gone, sliding heavily off the counter and excavating my jacket from the pile on a kitchen chair.

"I suspect," Greer said brightly, still sitting up on the counter, "that the feeling is mutual."

"You're picking that up too, right?" I asked. "I mean, don't get me wrong, I'm not whining about getting hazed or whatever—"

"Aren't you?" Greer teased.

"I'm not!" I insisted. "It just feels, like, personal, that's all. Don't you think that seemed kind of personal?"

Greer shook her head. "Hunter's just like that."

"I guess." I looked down at her knee for a second, feeling my eyebrows crawl. "How well do you guys know each other?"

"I mean, not that well," she said with a shrug. "Just enough to know he's—"

"A real dick?"

"Exactly," she said with a grin.

"Yeah." I sighed, shrugging into my jacket. "Anyway. I'm gonna go take care of this. I'll see you when I get back?"

But Greer shook her head. "I'm gonna go collect Bri and drag her out of here in a minute," she said. "I've got a response paper due at midnight. I want to read it one more time before I send it in."

I nodded, knowing better than to ask whether that was necessary. Greer's first year at Harvard hadn't gone super, from the sound of it. She'd told me bits and pieces of the story in passing—a stats teacher who'd had it in for her, a couple of big assignments she'd whiffed—but the upshot was that she was on academic probation this semester, which meant if she didn't pull her grades up by Christmas she was done. "Tomorrow, then?"

Greer tilted her dark, glossy head to the side. "Maybe," she agreed slowly. "What did you have in mind?"

"I mean, I don't know," I said, not wanting to sound as eager as I knew I probably did. "Walking tour of the Freedom Trail, maybe."

"Take a ride on a duck boat."

"Visit the USS *Constitution*," I joked. Then, dropping my voice a little, not quite looking at her: "We could always blow off all our classes, go to the beach for the day."

Greer snorted. "You realize it's going to be like fifty degrees."

"We'll wear sweaters," I countered easily—enjoying myself now, glad to have settled back into a rhythm with her and hoping she was glad about it too. We'd had fun together, a million years ago. It had been good, what we were. "Take our shoes off. It'll be like a Nicholas Sparks movie, we can do the whole thing."

That made her smile. "Tempting," she admitted, "but not really an option for me at this particular academic juncture. I'm done at noon, though. Why don't you come by the suite and I'll swipe you into the dining hall at Hemlock?"

"You sort of lack a romantic imagination," I informed her. "Do you know that about yourself?"

Greer nodded seriously. "I have been told that in the past, yes."

"I guess I forgive you," I decided.

"That's very generous."

"I'm a generous guy," I told her, "as evidenced by the fact that I guess I am about to go buy beer for the entire Harvard University lacrosse team and fifty of their closest friends." I gestured grandly toward the back door of the lax house. "Wish me luck."

"Oh yeah," Greer said with a laugh, "you're embarking on a regular hero's journey out there."

"I am." I stepped cautiously between her knees, dropping my hands lightly onto her denim-covered thighs and hoping my touch was more welcome to her than Hunter's had been. "Who knows what could happen to me?"

"Who knows," Greer echoed, her full mouth twisting in amusement. She always wore cherry ChapStick, Greer; she kept tubes of it everywhere, in her coat pockets and desk drawers and in the zippered compartment of the vintage neon Jansport she'd carried back at Bartley. After we broke up I found one in the pocket of my favorite jeans, though not before I'd put them through the dryer and melted bright pink wax onto almost every article of clothing I owned.

"Linden," she said now, peeling my hands off her legs, lacing her fingers through mine.

"Greer."

Just for a second, she leaned forward; I closed my eyes like an instinct, but in the end she just used me for leverage, sliding neatly off the counter and slipping past me in the direction of the living room. "I'll see you tomorrow, okay?"

"Yeah," I promised, swallowing down a warm-beer gulp of disappointment. It had been like this since we'd first started hanging out again, a tacit push-pull I wasn't quite sure how to read. It wasn't that Greer didn't seem interested, exactly. It was more like she was holding me off just to see if I'd wait. "See you tomorrow."

Outside, it was purple-dark and chilly, the wind rustling the branches of the oak trees overhead. Six blocks away, there was a corner deli that sold beer and reliably didn't look too hard at IDs, which was important, since mine said I was a twenty-six-year-old organ donor from Raynham named Danylo Rukaj. I headed in that direction, then stopped and glanced back at the lax house for a moment, squinting at the yellow light glowing behind the curtains and listening to the party going on without me. Then I pulled up my collar and set off.

2

Friday, 10/18/24

THE SUN WAS JUST STRETCHING ITS ARMS OVER THE
tops of the academic buildings when my alarm went off the following morning. I had a real first-year kind of schedule, with eight a.m.
classes every single morning of the week; on Fridays it was International Women Writers with Professor McMorrow, who was young-
ish and palpably brilliant, with a strict no-bullshit policy and a nose
like a blade. The second week of class, some finance major with a
two-hundred-dollar haircut had jumped in with a question that was
really more of a comment about what he described as *the wokening of
the Ivy League,* and I'd watched her take him out so cleanly she might
as well have been a resistance sharpshooter in 1942 Paris. Something
about her reminded me of my mom, actually, if my mom had gone
to graduate school at Yale and Oxford instead of meeting my dad
smoking a cigarette outside the Cantab in the spring of 2003.

"Nice work today, Michael," the professor said as I headed out
the door of the lecture hall. "But don't forget to message me to set
up a meeting, okay?"

I nodded. McMorrow was also my academic advisor, which meant that, per the email that had gone out to all first-year students at the beginning of the semester, I was supposed to have already scheduled a time to go to her office for a heart-to-heart about picking a major and fitting into the Harvard community and, presumably, what I wanted to be when I grew up. I wasn't sure why I kept putting it off, except for the fact that I didn't have answers to any of those questions, and one thing about the *Harvard community* was that everyone else decidedly did. "I will," I promised. "I'll do it tonight."

I had another class in a different building immediately after that one, and by the time it was done I was starving, so I grabbed a Snickers bar from one of the vending machines and ate it in two big bites, dry leaves crunching under my sneakers as I crossed campus toward Hemlock House. Greer's dorm was vintage Harvard, a big old brick building with a slate roof and a dozen chimneys, all narrow hallways and windows that didn't open properly and a geriatric elevator of questionable repute. I'd seen three different mice—at least, I *thought* they were three different mice; I suppose it could have been one particularly industrious mouse on three different occasions—in the handful of times I'd been inside.

My key card didn't give me access to any dorm other than my own, but a girl in jeans and a cable knit sweater held the front door open for me as she was leaving—an unsmiling blond who looked vaguely familiar, though I wasn't sure from where. I'd met a lot of people during orientation back at the beginning of the semester, when every social interaction felt like it began with someone in a brightly colored T-shirt announcing a game of Two Truths and a Lie (*I'm originally from East Boston, I'm allergic to apples, two summers ago I helped solve a murder; no, I'm not allergic to apples*). Since then I'd mostly hung out with the guys I knew from the lax team—and, more recently, with Greer.

She lived on the fourth floor of Hemlock, in a six-person suite made up of three doubles surrounding a small common space with a bathroom and a kitchenette. The girls usually kept the main door propped open with a book or a shower shoe wedged underneath it, and I knocked twice before I let myself inside. "Hey!" I called, breathing in the same burned-popcorn smell that all the suites had, cut by a faint whiff of hair product and a cupcake-scented plug-in. The common room was empty, somebody's crusty bowl of mac and cheese sitting forlornly on the coffee table. "Are you here?"

"Um, hi!" Greer called from the direction of her bedroom, her voice pitched a little higher than normal. "Yeah."

"Hey," I said again, heading down the dimly lit hallway. Greer's room—her side of it, at least—reminded me a lot of the one she'd lived in back at Bartley: thoughtfully considered and immaculately tidy, the bed made up with an antique quilt from Etsy and a Mark Rothko poster tacked neatly to the wall above the desk. Toni Morrison and *The Tempest* lined the bookshelf alongside a couple of the frothy, brightly covered romances Greer didn't like to admit she read, a vintage Polaroid camera serving as a bookend. The photos themselves were tucked into a ribbon board beside the bed, Greer with her parents in front of the big Christmas tree in New York City and a close-up of Bri at last year's spring formal, her red lips puckered like Marilyn Monroe's. Sweaters hung neatly in the closet. Jewelry hung neatly on hooks. *A place for everything,* I could almost hear Greer's mother telling her. *Everything in its place.*

Well. That was how it usually looked.

"Whoa," I said now, stopping short in the doorway. The whole room was a mess, the floor strewn with books and burrito wrappers and party clothes, like a panicky ghost had ransacked the wardrobe before dashing outside stark naked for a night of haunting. The drawers were all hanging open. The trash can had been overturned. "What happened?"

Greer shook her head. "I have no idea," she said, looking around at the damage. She was standing in the center of the room, holding a T-shirt she must have randomly scooped off the floor, her expression bewildered. "I just got back from class and it was like this." She rolled her eyes. "Probably Bri looking for her last party pill she thought she dropped somewhere, let's be honest with ourselves."

"Really?" I asked, unconvinced. The room did not *seem* to me like it had been tossed by Bri looking for her last party pill she thought she dropped somewhere, but it didn't seem immediately wise to say that out loud. "Is anything, like, missing?"

"I mean—" Greer looked around a little uncertainly, seeming to falter for a moment. "I don't think so?"

"Do you want me to get the RA?"

"What? *No.*" She shook her head, coming back to herself, though the color was still high in her cheeks. "What for, to tell her that Bri is a slob? It's fine. I'll make her buy me brunch this weekend, that's all."

"Okay," I said, gingerly setting my backpack down on the floor in the hallway, feeling pretty sure that there was more going on here than Greer was saying but not exactly sure what it might be. Girls could be kind of animals sometimes, I knew that about them. One time back at Bartley I'd seen a pair of roommates send each other to the ER. "Well, I can help you pick it up, at least."

"Are you sure?" Greer asked, frowning a little. "You definitely don't have to."

"No, of course," I said quickly. "Are you kidding? I'm about to spend my entire weekend scouring the grout at the lax house with a Magic Eraser. This is nothing."

That made her smile. "Okay," she agreed. "If you're sure."

"Greer," I said softly. "I'm sure."

We worked in companionable silence for a while, folding and sorting and setting things to rights. It felt weirdly intimate touching Greer's stuff like this, lining up the perfume bottles on her dresser and fluffing the throw pillows on her bed. Greer filched a dustbuster from one of her suitemates' rooms, running it over the rug for good measure. "Good enough," she decided finally, sitting down on the edge of the mattress and running her hands through her hair. "Thanks, Linden."

"Yeah, sure thing." I hesitated for a moment, then sat down in the desk chair. "No big deal."

"No, it is a big deal," Greer countered. "You're a good guy, you know that? I forgot that about you. Or, like, I tried to."

I glanced at her sidelong, grinning a little. "I can't tell if that's a compliment or not."

"It's a compliment," she promised, reaching out and nudging

me in the ankle with one white platform sneaker. "I missed you, is what I'm telling you here. Take the win."

"Okay," I agreed. "I missed you too."

"Did you?" she asked. "Say more about that." Then, when I only mumbled noncommittally: "Oh, come on." Her voice was warm and familiar, the sound of the heat clanking on in the dorms back at Bartley. "It's a little late to get shy, good buddy."

"I'm not *shy*," I said, though I was, a little bit. She undid me, Greer. She always had. "I might have checked your Instagram once or twice last year, who can say."

"Who indeed," Greer echoed teasingly. "This was in between you running up and down the Eastern Seaboard hooking up with a million other girls, yes?"

"I wasn't hooking up with a million girls," I protested, though I was secretly a little pleased she cared enough to be jealous. In fact, I'd hooked up with exactly one girl since Greer—but barely, and only just before she announced with zero equivocation that she never wanted to see me again as long as she lived. She was at Sarah Lawrence now, or that was the rumor; she'd blocked me on all social media platforms, so I couldn't confirm.

"That's not what I heard," Greer said now, taking my hand and tugging me over onto the bed beside her.

"Well, you heard wrong." I raised my eyebrows, leaning back against the wall. "Why, were you asking around about me?"

She shrugged. "I may have been."

"Say more about *that*."

"I don't think I will, actually."

"Hardly seems fair."

"It doesn't, does it."

"Can I ask you something?" I blurted before I could lose my courage, looking at her in the autumn light seeping in through the tall, narrow window, dim even though it was still midday. "What exactly happened between us? After the accident, I mean. It was like one second we were fine, we were *good,* and then suddenly after . . ."

It was the first time either one of us had mentioned it since I'd gotten to campus, and it took Greer a moment to answer. "I don't know," she admitted finally, pulling her feet up onto the edge of the wooden bed frame, wrapping her arms around her knees. "I just felt so guilty after everything that happened, you know? I basically ruined your entire life, Linden."

"You didn't," I said immediately. "You didn't."

"I mean, maybe not in reality," Greer pointed out. "It turned out okay. But like . . . it definitely felt that way at the time. It *did,*" she insisted when I started to protest. "You were hobbling around campus in so much pain, you couldn't play lacrosse, you were so angry and so miserable—"

"So you thought you'd just cut your losses and ditch me?" It was out before I could stop it.

"I didn't *ditch* you, Linden!" Greer sounded wounded. "You barely had two words to say to me, don't you remember that? Every time we were together it was like this heavy, malignant fog hanging between us. This fucked-up thing had happened, and it was all my fault." She shrugged. "I guess I thought the best way to handle it was just to leave you alone and let you live your life."

"Greer," I started, though even as I opened my mouth to contradict her I knew she wasn't wrong. As a general rule I tried not to think about the weeks after the accident, the way I couldn't run or climb stairs or even shower without help. I'd spent ten days back at my mom's house, where all I did was have doctors' appointments and watch television and wait for it to be time to take my meds. I was furious. I was terrified. It was like there was poison leaking out of my pores. "I'm sorry."

"*I'm* sorry," she countered. "For all of it."

"It was an accident," I reminded her, though truthfully there was a part of me that wondered if maybe it had all been avoidable. Greer had never told me the full story of what we'd been doing out there on the road that night, and I'd always been too afraid to push her; even now, it didn't feel like the right moment to ask. "And it all turned out okay."

Greer looked over at me then, her shoulder warm against me, her mouth close enough to kiss. "It did, huh?"

"It did."

Greer grinned. "Come on," she said, springing to her feet and taking me with her, pulling me gently toward the door. "I'm done for the day, and I vaguely remember somebody saying something about a beach walk. And I will tell you, Linden: suddenly, I seem to be finding myself in a Nicholas Sparks sort of mood."

"Duly noted," I said, lacing my fingers through hers and squeezing. Glancing over my shoulder one more time before we left.

In the end we took the bus to Castle Island, eating paper cups of French fries from Sully's and dodging seagulls so big and mean they looked like omens. The wind was freezing cold against my face. It was nearly dark by the time we got back to Cambridge, Greer's chilly hand slipping into mine as we made our way across campus toward Hemlock. I could hear an old Lorde song drifting out somebody's open window, the tinkling ring of a bell on a passing bike.

"You have plans for tonight?" Greer asked, our index fingers still hooked together even as she walked backward up the wide stone steps in front of the building. "Or do you maybe want to come up for a bit?"

"I can come up," I said a beat too quickly, my heart turning over once inside my chest. "Yeah, of course I can come up."

"Okay," Greer said, and the smile that spread across her face was slow and knowing. "Well then. Come up."

I followed her through the lobby of Hemlock and up the winding staircase, breathing in the cold city smell coming off her, the ends of her hair just brushing against my face. I was imagining the two of us alone in her room, her bare skin golden in the glow of the Christmas lights tacked up above the windows, but when she opened the door to her suite, all five of her suitemates were sprawled like sirens across the furniture in the common room— the TV blaring, the smell of nail polish sharp in the air.

"Oh!" I said before I could stop myself, unable to keep the disappointment out of my voice. Margot was eating Cup Noodles while Celine painted little yellow happy faces onto her toenails;

Bri tapped away on her laptop as Keiko scrolled industriously through her phone. "Uh. Hey, guys."

Dagny looked at me from where she was sitting cross-legged on the floor with a blanket over her shoulders like a cape, her lips quirking faintly. "Hey yourself." She raised an eyebrow at Greer. "Please tell me you didn't bring a dude to Richard Gere pregame."

"I mean, not just *any* dude," Greer protested, shrugging out of her jacket and draping it playfully over Dagny's head. "It's Linden. He barely counts."

"Uh, hang on," I said. "Putting a pin in *that* charming bit of personal description for a minute: What's Richard Gere pregame?"

"Pretty much exactly what it says on the tin, Big Harvard," Greer explained with a grin. She crossed the common room to the kitchenette and pulled a couple of clementines and a bag of Halloween candy down off the shelf before wriggling onto the love seat next to Bri. "Every Friday night we pregame to a different Richard Gere movie—"

"Although sometimes we don't actually make it out after," Bri explained, "because the act of participating in Richard Gere pregame reminds us that we don't actually like most people besides each other and Richard Gere."

"I like Richard Gere more than I like you guys," Celine piped up. "To be clear."

"Understood," Greer promised.

"Entered into the record," Margot agreed.

"Anyway," Greer continued, her expression all mischief when she looked back in my direction, "we're doing *An Officer and a*

Gentleman tonight, though I guess it's possible I forgot to mention that when I invited you up here? I can't really remember. Of course, if it doesn't sound like a good time to you . . ." She trailed off.

"Uh-huh." I nodded slowly, gazing at the six of them for a moment, their sweatpants and their ponytails and their barely contained amusement. They looked like sisters from a fairy tale. They looked like a flock of dangerous birds. "Richard Gere pregame sounds great."

Greer smiled at that, holding a clementine out in my direction. "It does, doesn't it?" she asked, scooting closer to Bri to make room for me. I sat down beside her, wedging myself into the corner of the too-small love seat. Taking the fruit from her hand.

3

Saturday, 10/26/24

I WENT FOR A LONG RUN MOST SATURDAY MORNINGS that fall, looping my way through the quiet streets of Cambridge or over the BU bridge and down into the crowded pedestrian bustle of Back Bay. It was the weekend before Halloween, and Harvard Square was full and festive, cotton cobwebs hanging in the store windows and little kids wandering around dressed as superheroes and spies. There were hundreds of jack-o'-lanterns stacked on risers on Cambridge Common, ready to be lit as part of a festival that night.

My stomach growled as I turned off Mass Ave and back onto campus—I usually ate with my roommates on the weekends, the three of us jostling each other in line for the waffle maker in the dining hall downstairs. I liked Dave and Duncan a lot, generally, though I knew they were both angling for an invitation to the lax house one of these nights and were starting to wonder why I hadn't delivered. It wasn't that I was embarrassed by them, though back at Bartley I probably would have been: the earnestness of them, their jokey T-shirts and Axe body spray and utter lack of guile. None of that felt like it mattered nearly as much here as it had in high school, in general, but still every time I opened my mouth to ask them to tag along I imagined Hunter catching sight of them across the room like a poacher snagging a pair of baby elephants in the crosshairs of his rifle, and figured I was doing them both a favor by acting like I didn't know they wanted to come.

"Hey," I said now, pushing the door of our room open. "Do you guys want to—"

I broke off, stopping short: Holiday Proctor was sitting in my desk chair, her feet up on my desk like the villain in a James Bond movie.

"Shit," I said, my shoulders dropping.

"You forgot," she accused.

"I didn't forget," I protested.

"Uh-huh." Holiday wasn't buying. "You know, I literally thought, *Just this once, I'm not going to send Michael a reminder that we made plans to hang out, and he is fully going to blank it.*"

"Does it get exhausting, being right all the time?"

"You'd think so," she said sweetly, "but actually I find it quite invigorating."

"I forgot a little," I admitted, guilt prickling warmly at the back of my neck. "But I'm really happy you're here."

"I'm sure you are," she said seriously. Then her face split open into a grin. She hopped up out of the chair and threw her arms around me, hugging me so tight she nearly knocked me over. "Hi," she said.

"Hi." I closed my eyes for a second before I quite knew I was going to do it, breathing in the familiar smell of tea and incense and weed. She was wearing high-waisted jeans and a sweater that was oversized even on her tall, broad frame, her riot of dark, curly hair loose and wild around her face.

I probably would have held on a minute longer—we'd barely seen each other since school started, and I was surprised to realize just how much I'd missed her—but all at once I realized Duncan and Dave were sitting on their respective bunk beds, trying with various degrees of subtlety to act like they weren't paying attention. "How'd you even get into the building?" I asked Holiday, stepping back and tucking my hands into my hoodie pocket. I'd seen her talk her way into a lot of places in the decade and a half we'd known each other, though our dorm had a desk attendant downstairs who was in theory supposed to prevent randos from just strolling on in without a key card.

"I've got a couple of friends from Greenleaf who live here," Holiday explained, naming the artsy private high school where she'd graduated the previous spring. Holiday was getting her BFA in musical theater across the river at Emerson, where I liked to imagine everyone walked around reciting Shakespeare and singing selections from *Wicked,* the click-clack of a million manual typewriters echoing through the corridors at all hours of the day and night. "I took advantage of their hospitality, since yours was—"

"Nonexistent?" I grimaced.

"You're fine." Her voice was high with the slightest lilt of mocking, but her smile was sincere, the warmth of it like a fire crackling in the lobby of a house you'd walked all day to get to. "Your roommates and I are old friends at this point. I think Duncan and I are going to go on vacation together."

"Turks and Caicos," Duncan agreed, his round cheeks gone nearly as red as his rusty mop of hair. He was a math major, with a slightly panicky smile and a bright green Yeti water bottle he carried everywhere like a security blanket; he'd been trying to grow a beard since our first week on campus, with a limited amount of success. "Maybe Mallorca."

"Mallorca sounds nice," Holiday agreed. "Dave, what do you think about Mallorca?" She turned back to me as Dave shot her an enthusiastic thumbs-up, eyes still trained on his laptop. "Michael's not invited, obviously."

"Probably for the best," I reminded her. "You know I burn easy."

"You're delicate," Holiday concurred.

We said our goodbyes to the guys and stopped by the fancy doughnut shop in the student center, where all the doughnuts cost four dollars each and had flavors like lychee and fresh-cut grass, then wandered down to the river to eat. It was warm that day, and the trees lining either side of the river all exploding in brilliant yellows and golds. Holiday slipped her shoes off, wriggling her painted toes in the coarse city grass as she flopped onto her back and closed her eyes. "I know this weather is because of global warming," she said. "But also, this weather is the absolute shit."

"It doesn't suck," I agreed, my phone buzzing in my pocket as

I sat beside her. When I glanced down I had a text from Duncan: *Hey Linden,* he'd written, which was how he began all his texts to me, *does Holiday have a boyfriend?*

I frowned as a bright flicker of annoyance zipped through my body, a weird current of irritation I didn't want to examine too closely. It wasn't like I cared who Holiday hooked up with, though she did have notoriously miserable taste in guys: when I'd gotten back to Boston for winter break last year, she'd been dating some guy from Buckingham, Browne & Nichols who looked like he was about to star in a prestige television drama as the art school son of a billionaire who got a solo show at a fancy gallery by dunking his penis in paint and slapping it on a canvas a bunch of times. Suffice it to say I wasn't that bummed out about it when they broke up right before graduation. She and I had actually wound up spending most of the summer together in the aftermath: I had a job shelving library books at the Eastie branch of the BPL, while she taught acting and stage combat to a bunch of little kids at the performing arts camp she'd attended all through elementary school. It had been a good time, Holiday picking me up most afternoons in her filthy Honda and the two of us dicking around Boston, going to all-ages shows at the Paradise and doing an exhaustive raspberry-lime rickey taste test and watching the sunset on the Esplanade. It had never been anything but platonic—Holiday and I had been friends since we were in preschool, and that was all—but still, I didn't like the idea of Duncan sniffing around.

Don't be gross, I typed now, then shoved my phone back inside my pocket and plunked myself down on the grass.

"What?" Holiday asked, propping herself up on both elbows and turning to look at me.

"Nothing."

"You're scowling."

"Am I?"

"You are."

"Pretty sure that's just how my face is."

"Pretty sure it's not," she fired back, but she let it go, dropping down onto her back one more time. "Also: you smell."

"*You* smell," I countered immediately. "I was running."

"Uh-huh." She grinned. "What are you up to tonight?" she asked, stretching her arms above her head, her sweater riding up a little bit so I caught a glance of her pale, soft stomach. "Is there a Halloween thing?"

I nodded, looking away. "Lacrosse party."

"Ah," she said. "Right."

"What?"

"Nothing," she said. "It just seems like maybe you're doing a lot of that here, that's all."

"I mean, to be fair, I've also occasionally been attending my first semester of classes at Harvard University."

"Ever heard of it?" she teased.

"I'm serious!" I protested. "I'm here on a lacrosse scholarship, Holiday. I kind of have to hang out with the team."

"No, I know you do," she agreed. "I just forgot for a second how *get crunked with my bros* was right there in the list of the requirements next to showing up for practice and maintaining a three point five GPA."

"First of all, it's three point six," I said. "Second of all, it's part of being on the—it's a whole—" I broke off. "You know that."

"I do," Holiday said. "I know that."

I sighed. It was like this sometimes, with Holiday—she and I had been best friends for basically our entire childhoods, but we didn't talk for most of high school, and it wasn't until we ran into each other on Martha's Vineyard a couple of years ago that we got close again. It was complicated, sort of. On occasion, it had been known to get weird. "Okay," I said finally. "Then why are you looking at me like I shat on your carpet?"

Holiday's eyes narrowed behind the big round frames of her glasses. "Maybe that's just how my face is."

"I think I know your face better than most people," I pointed out, taking a sip of my iced coffee.

Holiday shrugged into the grass. "Maybe," she admitted. There was something I didn't understand in her expression, just for a second; then she blinked and it was gone. "What are you even taking?" she asked instead, sitting up again and tucking one leg underneath her, pulling her doughnut out of its bag and plucking a sprinkle off the top. "Like, classwise, I mean."

I filled her in on Economic Justice and Race, Gender, and Performance, the advisor meeting I'd been putting off with Professor McMorrow. "I don't know," I said, watching as a thirtysomething couple in matching Chacos pushed an expensive-looking stroller along the walking path. "I told myself I'd get over my impostor-type bullshit once I got here, and I guess I mostly have? But it does kind of feel like everybody else has known exactly what they were going to do when they grew up since basically the day they were born."

Right away, Holiday shook her head. "Not everybody."

"You," I pointed out.

"I mean, sure, but who knows if I'm actually going to get to do it," she countered. "*Be on Broadway* is not exactly what one might call a rock-solid career aspiration. Let's be real, I'm probably going to wind up teaching theater games at a residential school for kids with violent behavioral problems."

"Doubtful," I said. I knew she didn't really think that, and she knew I knew she didn't; if there was one thing Holiday had never lacked, it was a clear-eyed confidence about exactly how much she was capable of. Still, I appreciated her saying it. "You'll go full EGOT."

"Well. That's very loving." Holiday pulled off a piece of her doughnut and popped it into her mouth. "Anyway," she said once she'd swallowed, "the point is, nobody knows exactly what they're going to wind up doing, and you shouldn't let anyone bully you into picking a major just to pick it. You're actually exactly the kind of person who should take some time before they declare."

I felt myself frown. "Meaning what, exactly? Why are you like, negging me today?"

"I'm not!" Holiday insisted, not especially convincingly; it occurred to me to wonder if maybe she wasn't quite as chill about me forgetting our plans as she'd pretended to be. "I'm just saying it would be good to look around and figure out what you actually like before you settle on some random thing just to have it decided."

"Good for me more than other people?"

"Good for all people equally," she promised, but then, a moment later, and more quietly: "I guess I just don't want you to waste your time here, that's all."

"Here, where?" That surprised me. "Like at college? Waste it how?"

"Well, think about it," she instructed. "Two summers ago on the Vineyard your ankle was still hamburger. You couldn't play. You didn't even know if you were going to be able to finish out high school at Bartley, let alone get a scholarship to college. And now—look at you, Michael. Like you just said, you're literally at Harvard. Even adjusting for privilege and general douchebaggery, you're surrounded by some of the most brilliant and interesting minds of our whole entire generation." She shrugged. "I just don't want you to spend the next four years hanging out with the exact same guys you hung out with for the last four, that's all."

"And who *should* I be hanging out with, exactly?" I asked, trying to keep my voice light, to ignore the uncomfortable prickle of recognition I felt at what she was saying. That was the problem with Holiday, forever and always: she saw everyone, me especially, a little too clearly for comfort. "Actors?"

Holiday grinned. "I mean," she said with a theatrical preen, "you could do worse."

I smiled back, though something about the conversation irked me—Holiday slipping so easily into the role of my slightly snotty big sister, maybe, even though we were exactly the same age. My mom had worked for the Proctors at their big house near Porter Square basically since I was in diapers, cooking their meals and dusting their bookshelves and driving Holiday to her various fencing matches and modern dance rehearsals and auditions for community theater productions of *Funny Girl*. We weren't siblings, but we might as well have been.

Possibly, Holiday could sense that I was feeling prickly, because she deftly changed the subject to an improv performance some friends of hers were doing in the park the following afternoon, and the conversation wandered from there, our fingers sticky with doughnut glaze as we watched the last rowers of the season make their way down the Charles. We covered dining hall food and the religious zealot who liked to hand out pamphlets on Brookline Avenue and how all the good stores in Harvard Square had turned into banks now, and it wasn't until I mentioned a Netflix show Greer had told me to watch that Holiday frowned. "Oh!" she said, digging busily around in the doughnut bag and handing me a napkin. "I didn't realize that was a thing that was happening again. You and Greer, I mean."

"Kind of." I lifted an eyebrow, feeling briefly like I'd gotten caught doing something illicit. "Why, is that a problem?"

"No," Holiday said immediately, balling up the wax-paper bag. "Of course not. I just—no." She shook her head, then pulled her phone out of her enormous, perpetually overstuffed tote and wrinkled her nose at the time. "It's late," she announced suddenly, though in fact it was the middle of the afternoon and broad daylight. "I gotta get back."

In the end I decided it was better not to press her, holding a hand out to pull her to her feet. The Square was crowded with tourists as I walked her back toward the T station, the *Ghostbusters* theme song blaring from the open windows of an Uber passing by. "What are *you* doing tonight?" I asked. "Like, a reading of *Macbeth* in a graveyard by candlelight?"

"Some of the people in my cohort are putting on an Edgar Allan Poe thing, if you must know," Holiday reported tartly. "Then *Rocky Horror* at Coolidge Corner at midnight."

"Obviously." Holiday had always loved a midnight movie; over the summer she'd dragged me to half a dozen of them, *Jurassic Park* and *Aliens* and something called *A Gnome Named Gnorm* from which I still had not entirely recovered. We spent most of that one drinking thermoses of rum punch out of her purse, only then I spilled mine into her lap and when she jammed a kernel of popcorn in my ear in retaliation, part of it got stuck in there. She'd needed to use tweezers and the flashlight on her phone to get it out.

"You could blow off your party and come, you know," she told me now, raising her voice as she walked backward toward the entrance to the train station. "Meet some different kinds of people, even. Really immerse yourself in the theater sce—"

"Goodbye, Holiday!"

Holiday grinned at me, her smile luminous in the late-season sunlight. "See you around, Michael."

4

Saturday, 10/26/24

BACK AT MY DORM I GRABBED DINNER AND A SHOWER, then sat on my bed and pulled my phone out of my pocket, flicking through my contacts until I got to Greer's name. *See you at the lax house tonight?* I asked, hoping I sounded appropriately casual and not like I'd spent the better part of six miles composing and revising this exact text in my head on my run earlier today.

The phone buzzed with her reply a moment later: *I can't,* Greer reported, adding a little sad face emoji. *I have a biochem quiz first thing Monday morning. Going to get a PSL as big as my head and go work in the library like the most basic of bitches.*

On Halloween weekend? I couldn't help but ask.

I know, she texted back. *The worst. But my dad wants to schedule a Zoom to talk about the "outlook for the remainder of the semester," which is honestly scarier to me than the Babadook at this point.*

I flopped back onto the mattress, fighting down an embarrassing surge of disappointment. *That sucks,* I typed, for lack of anything clever or useful to say. *Breakfast tomorrow, maybe?*

"So hey," Duncan said just then, leaning back in his desk chair across the room. His voice was so, so casual. There was a tiny hole in the bottom of his sock. "About your friend Holiday."

I felt my eyes narrow. "What about her?"

"You guys aren't . . ." Duncan frowned, reaching for his water bottle and cradling it like a newborn baby. "I mean, are you?"

"We aren't what, exactly?"

"He wants to know if you guys have boned," Dave piped up helpfully, "but he's afraid you'll beat him up for asking."

That stopped me. "When have I ever acted like I was going to beat either one of you up for anything?" I asked, weirdly wounded. "Like, is that the vibe I give off to people?"

"I'm not afraid you're going to beat me up," Duncan clarified.

I frowned. "I thought we were friends."

"Are we?" Dave asked. He tilted his head, his straight black hair falling across his eyes. "Like, is that what you would call us?"

"Yes!" This was absurd. "Anyway, to answer your question, no, of course not. We've never—" I shook my head. "She's like my sister."

"To be fair, I don't think he'd want you to date his *sister* either," Dave pointed out, munching a Bugle on the bottom bunk.

"That's not the poi— Look, I gotta go," I announced abruptly, getting up off the bed and yanking a clean shirt over my head, screwing with my hair in the mirror on the back of the closet door. "I'll see you guys in the morning, all right? Don't forget to check your Halloween candy for needles."

I met up with George Patel and a handful of other first-years for the pregame in a different dorm across campus, where I drank three beers a little faster than I meant to, so my head was already feeling like a balloon by the time we headed over to the party. The lax house was warm inside: the steady thump of a bassline, the smell of booze and people and weed hanging densely in the air.

I got swallowed up into the crowd pretty much immediately, downing another couple of beers and playing wingman for George as he tried to make it happen with a girl from his Intro to Computer Science class. I was hoping Greer might have blown off the library and come anyway, that I'd catch sight of her perched on the steps, dressed as a black cat or a Freudian slip, but when I looked around the crowded living room there was no sign of her glossy dark hair and round tortoiseshell glasses. A few of her suitemates were here, though, and I waved to Keiko and Bri, who—judging by her rosy cheeks and slightly glassy expression—had also gotten her own personal party started at some point before she arrived.

"Linden!" she called when she spotted me, holding out her arms like we were long-lost sisters from a Disney movie. "Come settle a bet."

"Uh-oh," I said, weaving through the crowd. She was sitting on the arm of the couch with her shoes on the cushion, her sharp heels snagging on the worn leather. "What's up?"

Keiko was shaking her head. "Nothing," she assured me, nudging Bri with one sharp elbow. "We were just . . . speculating, that's all."

"About?" I asked, and both of them burst out laughing.

"Never mind," Keiko said firmly, though her gaze flicked unmistakably to my crotch before finding its way back up to my face. "Where's your costume?"

"Where's *yours*?" I countered, looking at Bri.

"This is it," she said, gesturing down at her outfit, jeans and a silky emerald-green tank top I was pretty sure belonged to Greer. "I'm a chameleon."

"Do you change colors?"

"Only when I get excited," she chirped, then turned back to Keiko. "Linden doesn't do Halloween costumes," she reported. "He's too cool."

"Is that what Greer told you?" I asked.

Bri's lips twisted. "Don't fish," she said primly. Then she grinned. She had a nice smile, Bri, warm and open. "She wants to get back together with you," she confessed, dropping her voice a little. "Greer, I mean."

Right away, Keiko shook her head. "I'm not hearing this!" she announced, sliding off the couch in the direction of the keg. "I know nothing."

"She wouldn't care if I told him!" Bri called after her. "They dated for like a full year!"

"She does?" I asked, trying not to sound too thirsty. "How can you tell?"

Bri shrugged. "She's my best friend. I know things."

"Well." I tucked my hands into my pockets. "For the record: I want to get back together with her too."

"Oh, we know," Bri assured me. "You're gonna have to nut up a little, though."

I snorted, hoping she wouldn't notice my cheeks reddening. "I'm trying."

"Try harder," she advised seriously. "She had a tough year last year, you know? For a lot of reasons. She needs something good in her life right now."

"I will . . . take that under consideration," I promised, sitting down beside her on the couch. "How's your semester going?"

Bri shrugged. "I don't know," she said, suddenly looking more sober than I'd ever seen her. "Good, I guess. I mean, my classes are fine." She was a double major, I knew, criminology and prelaw. "And I love living in the suite, obviously. But like, do you ever just look around this place and think, *What the fuck am I doing here with all these people?* I mean, don't get me wrong, my dad sells SUVs in Connecticut, you know? I'm not saying I grew up on the mean streets. But there's a girl in my Economic Justice seminar who's a literal countess. A countess! And also, not for nothing, she's a fuckin' bitch."

That made me laugh. "I get it," I said.

"I know you do," Bri said. I wondered what she meant by that, wondered what Greer might have told her. Back at Bartley I'd done everything I could to hide who I was and where I came from, a scholarship kid with a chip on his shoulder. I'd promised myself I wasn't going to do that here, but still, it was hard to ignore that instinctive flash of defensiveness, the impulse to protect the soft places.

We talked for a long time—about our classes and my roommates and her sister, who was in treatment for an eating disorder down in Stamford. I liked Bri, I couldn't help it. She reminded me of the girls I'd known back at Bartley: warm and witty and a little bit wild, always sharper than they first let on.

"Anyway," she said finally—or started to, then broke off to let out a small, ladylike burp. "Fuck me, that's my cue," she admitted with a laugh, listing a little as she got to her feet. "I gotta go."

"Fair enough," I said, holding out a hand to help her off the couch. "You okay to get home?"

"Oh yeah, I'm fine," she promised, waving to Keiko, who was sitting on the staircase next to a girl I vaguely recognized from the weight room at the gym. "I'll find a buddy. See you around, Linden."

The rest of the night passed in a blur: a sloppy game of Flip Cup, someone's beer spilled all over my sneakers. I was just about to see if there was anything to eat in the kitchen when someone called out across the living room. "Yo, Linden!" Here was Hunter, holding—oh, Jesus—a goldfish swimming frantically around in a drinking glass. "Got a little project for you."

I glanced around, suddenly and deeply uneasy. "What kind of project?" I asked, though there was a part of me that already knew.

Hunter held the glass out in my direction. "Bottoms up."

I could have said no, obviously. I could have told him to go fuck himself. It wouldn't have been the first time someone had done it: just this week another first-year, Oliver Beckett, had snapped and told Hunter to write his own fucking lit papers. It wasn't like he'd gotten kicked off the team. Still, there was a distinct coolness between Oliver and the rest of us now, underclassmen included. I hadn't seen him here at the party tonight.

That wasn't the only reason I wasn't about to back down, though. Back in elementary school I used to get in fights like all the time; I was small, and I got picked on a lot, and I had no dad to speak of, which was a good and efficient thing to make fun of me about if you were looking for a reaction. "Michael," my mom would say, dipping out of Holiday's parents' house to come pick me up in her ancient Toyota, parking me at their kitchen table to do my homework and demanding I not move, "I do not understand it. You know what you're supposed to do in a situation like that. Get a teacher. Walk away." I did know that, and I understood it; still, there was something about the challenge that felt irresistible to me. There was something satisfying about it, even when I knew there was no way it could possibly end well. I would one hundred percent always have rather taken the punch.

Now I lifted my chin in Hunter's direction, squared my shoulders, and took the glass from his outstretched hand. "Bottoms up," I echoed, and drank.

☜☞

It was almost three when I shuffled back across campus, the wind cold and biting. The temperature had dropped significantly; this afternoon by the river with Holiday felt like it had happened in a whole other life. The overnight security guard eyed me as I swiped my card to get into the building; a squirrelly-looking girl in a beanie smoked a cigarette near the gate.

I stumbled up the stairs and let myself into my room—we never bothered bolting the door, which was good because I couldn't have gotten the key into the lock if my life had literally depended on it. It took a moment for my eyes to adjust: Duncan was open-mouthed and snoring. Dave was watching *Emily in Paris* on his laptop. And sitting propped up on the pillows cross-legged in my bed, flicking lazily through her phone, was Greer.

"Hi," she said, smiling at me in the darkness. She was wearing cozy-looking sweatpants and a Harvard hoodie, her hair in a messy bun on top of her head.

"Hi." I blinked. The room was spinning wildly, and I flattened a hand against the wall to steady myself. "What are you doing here?"

Greer shrugged. "Checking to make sure you weren't bringing any other girls home," she deadpanned. "Also, I thought maybe you could use this." She reached over and plucked a plastic bottle of red Gatorade off the desk, holding it out in my direction.

"You're an angel," I told her. I think I did, anyway; like I said, I was pretty drunk. "I love you." Then I blanched. "I mean—you know what I mean. Don't freak out. I don't want you to freak out."

Greer shook her head, scooting over to make room for me on the mattress. "Go to sleep, dork," she said fondly. Her laughter was the last thing I heard before I fell asleep.

5

I WOKE UP FEELING LIKE SOMEONE WAS BORING DIrectly into my skull with a hammer drill, a taste in my mouth like the bottom of the Fort Point Channel. My stomach was roiling. My anxiety was cranked to ten.

"Morning, sunshine," Greer said with a smile. She was sitting pretzel-legged at the end of my bed, looking fresh as the bright yellow tulips that line the Public Garden in springtime. "Your roommates were going to wait for you for breakfast, but I told them it was probably going to be a while."

"I drank a goldfish," I told her sadly.

Greer nodded. "I know," she said, holding her phone up as evidence, waggling the video in my face. "I saw."

I winced, rolling over and burying my face in my too-warm pillow. "Oh, god."

"You're kind of viral," she informed me, in a voice that wasn't quite admiring. "Ten thousand views this morning already. You should see if you can leverage this somehow, maybe pick up a corporate sponsorship. I don't know with who, though." I could hear the smirk in her voice. "Like, definitely not Chewy dot-com."

I groaned into the mattress. "Am I a goldfish killer?"

"I mean, objectively, yes," she said, crawling back across the covers and tucking herself in beside me. She smelled like coffee and detergent and the fancy bespoke shampoo she bought off Instagram, which she used to carry to the bathroom at Bartley in a sleek little caddy. "But let's be real, if you didn't drink it, somebody else would have had to. That poor fucking goldfish never stood a chance."

"That's not really comforting to me, Greer."

"It wasn't meant to be," she said pleasantly, patting me on the back before sitting up one more time. "Now go take a shower. You smell like the floor of a bar."

We'd missed brunch in the dining hall entirely, so we walked up to a café near Porter Square for breakfast sandwiches. It was even chillier than the night before, and rainy, the leaves slick on the sidewalk and a wind that sliced cleanly through my jacket. Still, the cold air was bracing, and between that and the greasy bacon, egg, and cheese biscuit I inhaled in two enormous bites, I was feeling a full click steadier by the time we headed back to campus. "Good news," I reported, rattling the ice in my coffee cup. "I might live after all."

"That's a relief," Greer said, raising her elegant eyebrows. "And, you know. More than we can say for the fish."

I made a face. "Did you get your stuff finished last night?" I asked as she swiped her card outside of Hemlock House. I pulled the heavy wooden door open, nodding for her to go ahead. "Or do you have more to do today?"

"I literally always have more to do," Greer reported grimly, "but you can come up and keep me company while I do it, if you want. Or do some of your own, even."

I considered the dull throb of the hangover still echoing at the back of my skull. "That . . . might be ambitious." We crossed the black-and-white tile of the lobby, past the staircase that led down to the laundry room and a bulletin board bearing notices for STD testing at the health center and an a cappella concert of '90s boy band hits. "Did you do your Zoom with your dad?"

Greer shook her head. "His assistant sent me a calendar invite for Tuesday," she reported, "though I guess it's always possible I'll get listeria and die before then."

"Gotta manifest your dreams," I agreed as we climbed the spiral stairs to the fourth floor. "So, that's going super, huh? You and your parents, I mean." Greer's relationship with her family hadn't been great, back when we were at Bartley. Her mom and dad were what my old roommate Jasper had called *hardos,* meaning they were the kind of rich parents who cared a lot about grades and also never did cocaine, even on vacation.

"Oh yeah," Greer said with exaggerated carelessness. "It's amazing." She was quiet for a moment. "I mean, it's not that my parents don't love me. Like, they definitely love me? It's just that they don't always seem to *like* me that much."

"Really?" I frowned. "What's not to like?"

Greer smiled at that. "Why, thank you, Linden," she said, bumping her arm against mine. "I agree that I'm very charming."

"No," I said, stopping and taking her elbow, turning her gently so that she met my gaze. "I'm serious. You're literally at Harvard.

You're doing the thing. What else could they possibly want or expect?"

Greer shrugged, like it should have been obvious. "Greatness," she said simply.

I thought about my own mom, back across the river in Eastie. She'd always had high expectations, in her way: from the time I could walk she'd demanded I bus my own plate, clean up my own messes, save my own soul. Once, she signed me up for an entire weekend of community service because she saw me walk past an unhoused woman on the Common and not slip anything into her battered cup. Still, my mom had never, at any time, given me any indication whatsoever that she gave one single solitary shit either way about whether I played sports or where I went to college. I honestly don't think it had ever even occurred to her to wonder if I was great or not. The only thing she really cared about was that I was *good.*

And if sometimes it felt like that might have been a higher bar to clear, well, I suspected she probably knew that too.

Greer looked at me for a second, the two of us standing there in the stale dimness of the stairwell. In her glasses and her sweatpants, she looked very, very young. "Linden—" she started, then seemed to think better of it, turning and starting to climb one more time. "I mean," she said over her shoulder, her voice light and playful, "I think they also always kind of hoped I'd play the oboe."

Back in the suite, Keiko, Margot, Dagny, and Celine were all parked in the common room, the TV murmuring quietly and a small platoon of Starbucks cups scattered across the coffee table. Margot had her headphones on and was moving her lips silently, either practicing the conjugation of irregular verbs in Latin or listening to Taylor Swift on Spotify. Celine was eating Cinnamon Toast Crunch out of the box.

"Oh, *hello,*" Keiko said when we came in, her voice mock-formal. "Nice to see you." She looked at me pointedly, then back at Greer. "Is this what you meant when you said you were going to pull an all-nighter?"

"Rude," Greer replied primly. "How was everybody's evening?"

"I mean, nobody here drank a goldfish, if that's what you're asking." Keiko grinned at me. "How you feeling, Linden?"

"Full of shame and regret," I assured her.

"And goldfish," Greer said sweetly.

"Keiko hooked up with the drummer from the jazz quartet," Dagny reported.

"What? Shut up," Greer said, jaw dropping even as Keiko whacked Dagny with a throw pillow shaped like a slice of watermelon. "The girl with the septum piercing?"

"I didn't even think they let you *have* septum piercings at Harvard," Margot said, plucking a headphone from one ear.

I settled myself on one of the wobbly wooden stools at the breakfast bar, listening idly as they postgamed their respective Saturday night adventures, their voices rising and falling like a fugue they'd sung a million times before. I looked around the common room, thinking how different it was from the living room of the lax house, the way the girls had worked to make it feel like an actual home: they'd covered the college-issued couch with a crisp white sheet, laid the floor with a vintage rug I recognized from Greer's room back at Bartley. The overheads were off, a warm, cozy glow cast by a handful of mismatched lamps and a string of twinkle lights strung above the windows. Keiko was an art minor, and a triptych of her bright abstract paintings was tacked to the wall opposite the TV. "Bri still sleeping it off?" Greer asked finally, reaching out for the cereal box; Celine handed it over, wiping her sugary fingers on a fleecy throw blanket printed with stars.

"I think so," Keiko said. "She left the party with some girls from the crew team while I was, um, otherwise engaged. I haven't seen her."

"We hung out a little bit last night, actually," I reported helpfully, raising my eyebrows in Greer's direction. "She said you want to get back together with me."

"Oh, is *that* what she said?" Greer asked with a laugh, taking my hand and dragging me down the hallway toward her bedroom. "She must have been even more fucked up than usual."

The lights in Greer and Bri's room were blazing when she opened the door, though Bri was in fact passed out cold—sprawled on top of Greer's still-made bed in the same silky green chameleon top she'd been wearing at the party the night before, her dark hair a mess across the pillows.

"Big night," Greer said with a laugh, righting a lamp that was overturned on the desk, presumably where Bri had knocked it over as she stumbled and fumbled her way toward the closest available mattress. "Rise and shine, cupcake." She was reaching out to scratch Bri's back when suddenly her eyes narrowed; I followed her gaze, spying a small orange bottle and the remains of some crushed-up pills on the desk.

"Woof," I said, squinting at what was left of the label on the bottle—most of it had been scratched off, though a telltale *OXY* remained—even as Greer swore under her breath.

"What the fuck, Bri?" she muttered. "Is she trying to get us both kicked out of housing? Hey," she said, leaning down to shake Bri awake. "Can you please get up and get rid of this shit before we both wind up in jail?" Then she frowned. "Bri, babe," she said, shaking her a second time and then a third. "Bri?"

Greer gripped Bri's motionless shoulder, tugging her over onto her back before whirling to look at me, wild-eyed. "Is she breathing?" she asked, a full octave higher than normal. "I don't think she's breathing. Bri?"

"What?" I snapped to attention, my throat dropping into my stomach. Bri's mouth was slack, her skin horribly, unmistakably gray. Still: "Yes, she is," I said, full of useless bravado. "No, she definitely is."

"She's not." I could hear the fear rising in Greer's voice like a wave suddenly breaching the seawall. "She's *not.*"

"Call nine-one-one," I said, then bumbled my own phone out of my hoodie pocket even as Greer yelled down the hall to her suitemates.

What happened next was a blur, bright chaos and noisy panic: The girls flooded into Greer and Bri's room. Keiko dashed back out, yelling for help. A bespectacled RA came running, attempting clumsy CPR in the long minutes before the EMTs arrived with a couple of officers from Harvard's police department close behind them, their radios crackling with static as they shouted at the rest of us to give them room. The whole thing reminded me of another scene I'd witnessed two summers ago and a hundred miles from here: the purple predawn light of the beach in the early morning, a body floating motionless in a pool. That time, though, the paramedics had moved quickly and efficiently, careening away in the ambulance with lights and sirens blaring.

This time, I couldn't help but notice, they didn't seem to be in any hurry at all.

Greer noticed too. "Why aren't you helping her?" she demanded, the rest of us watching in slow-motion horror as one of the paramedics turned to his partner, shaking his head.

"I'm sorry," he said, and his voice was so quiet. "There's nothing we can do here."

❧

The afternoon seemed to go on forever. I sat with Greer while the police interviewed her and the rest of her suitemates, all of us clustered in the common room like some incredibly fucked-up family meeting. My hangover had returned with a vengeance, my stomach queasy, the headache pulsing brutally at the back of my eyeballs. "Did you know Bri was using drugs?" asked one of the officers, a tall, businesslike woman with glossy shoulder-length braids. "Or anything about where she might have gotten the pills?"

Greer shook her head. She looked dazed and bedraggled, her face raw and red from crying; her ponytail had mostly fallen out. "I mean, she went to a party at the lax house last night, but I don't know if that's where—" She broke off, her gaze cutting to me.

"Was that usual for her?" the other officer asked, a heavyset ginger with a spray of freckles who couldn't have been much older than us. "Excessive partying?"

"I didn't say it was excessive," Greer protested, looking to the other girls for backup. "I mean, she liked to have a good time, but—" She pressed the heels of her hands into her eyes. "I don't want to make it sound like she was some drug fiend. We're in college, you know? Especially a college like this—"

"But she used drugs and alcohol regularly?" the officer pressed.

"I—" Greer hesitated. "Yeah," she admitted grudgingly. "I guess."

"This party," the first officer put in. "You said it was with the lacrosse team?"

"Hang on a second," Dagny interrupted suddenly, holding a hand up. "Can I ask you a question? Do we need lawyers right now?"

"Why would you need lawyers?" the second officer asked, his expression even.

Dagny shrugged, her expression wary. "I mean, you tell me."

"It's fine, Dag," Margot said, pulling one leg up underneath her. She was the most composed of everyone, I'd noticed, the one who'd thought to put on a pot of coffee; the smell of it filled the suite now, comforting and warm. Keiko had spoken only when directly spoken to, while Celine, her arms wrapped around her knees on the love seat, hadn't said anything at all. "We want to be helpful, right?"

"Of course we want to be helpful," Dagny snapped, "but I'm also not about to call my mom and tell her I got expelled from

Harvard just because Bri bought fake Klonopin laced with horse tranquilizers, or whatever the hell—"

"Dagny!" Greer said. "Jesus."

I was expecting an argument, but right away Dagny's shoulders dropped, her whole body caving in on itself. "I'm sorry," she said, and that was when her voice broke. "Shit, I'm sorry. That was horrible. I'm sorry." Keiko slid an arm around her, pulling her close.

"Nobody's getting expelled," the first officer said, more gently now. "These things happen on campuses all the time, unfortunately. It's a tragedy. We just want to make sure we understand the chain of events."

Margot nodded. "Of course," she said, getting up and pouring Dagny a cup of coffee, pressing it into her shaking hands. "What do you need to know?"

Once they were finally gone—once the dean of students came and left and someone from down the hall dropped off dinner from Sugar & Spice and Keiko's dad drove in from Acton to try to take her home for the night, an offer she steadfastly refused—I carried Greer's pillow and blanket down the hall to Margot and Dagny's room, dropping her off there like she was a little kid going to a sleepover. "You sure you don't want me to stay?" I asked, hesitating in the doorway. "I can crash on the couch."

But Greer shook her head. "I'll be okay with these guys," she promised. "The RA said I can move out if I want to, but I don't want to leave the suite." She shrugged. "Kind of a fucked-up way to get a single, though." Her voice cracked then, and I watched as she sank onto the sofa, her shoulders shaking as she sobbed.

The rest of them were there before I could move in her

direction, all of them curling into one another, wrapping Greer up in their arms. They looked like a painting, piled together on the sofa: their fingers laced together, their heads in each other's laps.

I was extraneous here, obviously, so I said my goodbyes and headed across campus to my room, where Dave and Duncan were ostensibly doing homework but clearly actually waiting for me. "Dude," Duncan said by way of greeting, his voice low and serious, "this is so fucked up."

"Yeah," I said, feeling a little weird about the expectant way they were both looking at me. It's weird, the way a tragedy spreads through an ecosystem—the way everyone wants to process it out loud, to get close to it. *I almost knew this girl who died.* "It's pretty fucked up."

"So you were there when Greer found her?" Dave asked. "That's just, like—what people are saying."

"Uh, yeah," I said, flopping facedown onto my bed, then thinking of Bri sprawled on Greer's mattress and immediately getting up again. It felt like there were ants crawling all over my body. It felt like I'd never lie still again. "I was there."

"Dude," Duncan said again, still watching me. "So fucked up."

I nodded silently, biting back a surprising surge of temper. I liked living in a dorm, generally; I didn't have brothers or sisters, and usually it was a relief to me, the way there was always somebody to talk to. The way there was always somebody around. Right now, though? I kind of just wanted to be alone.

"I gotta run an errand," I announced, then shrugged back into my coat and went downstairs, shuffling across the Yard in the direction of the T stop, tapping my card and stepping onto the first inbound train that arrived. I thought about going home to Eastie and curling up on the sofa in my mom's apartment. I thought about showing up unannounced at Holiday's dorm. Instead, I just rode all the way to the end of the line and back again, staring out the window at the inside of the tunnel and listening to the noisy mechanical hum all around.

6

Tuesday, 10/29/24–Wednesday, 10/30/24

TIME PASSED STRANGELY IN THE WAKE OF BRI'S DEATH, stretching out like taffy before snapping tautly back again as the university machine whirred into gear. There were grief counselors available at the mental health center. A memorial service was planned for the end of the week. A campuswide call went out for remembrances of Bri to be published in an upcoming edition of the *Crimson*. "Great," Margot said when I mentioned it over dinner in the Hemlock dining hall on Tuesday, "so there's going to be a full-page spread of total strangers talking about how fun she was to party with."

"She was a straight-A student, for the record," Keiko piped up from across the table.

"She got into fucking Harvard!" Dagny shoved a dinner roll into her mouth.

It's not like I didn't understand why they were feeling protective. What happened to Bri had been the subject of all kinds of wild speculation on campus, rumors jumping like bedbugs from house to house: That she'd had a needle in her arm when Greer found her. That she'd sometimes traded blow jobs for coke. Even Cam, a person who could generally be relied upon to mind his business, had pulled me aside as we ran laps at the track early that morning to ask if it was true that Bri had gotten caught up in a hazing for a final club dabbling in dark rituals. "Of course not," I snapped, doubling my pace and pulling ahead of him. "This isn't the fucking Wizarding World of Who Gives a Fuck. Don't be a dumbass."

I was half expecting him to pop me in the face—and there was a part of me that almost wanted him to—but instead, he just stopped running, his expression wounded. "Aw, don't get mad, dude!" he called after me. "I was just double-checking!"

Even the faculty seemed to be after all the dirty details of Bri's death. When I checked my phone on the way back from dinner there was an email from Professor McMorrow reminding me I still hadn't scheduled my first-semester check-in. *Additionally,* she'd written, *a colleague mentioned you may have been friendly with the student who tragically passed away earlier this week. I wanted to let you know I'm here if you want to talk, either about that or about your semester more broadly. When might be a good time for us to meet?*

I scowled, shoving my phone back into my pocket as the lampposts blinked on all around me. "Nope," I muttered, though there was nobody around on the path to hear. "No, thank you. I'm good."

Bri's parents were scheduled to come pick up her stuff on Friday morning after the memorial service, so on Wednesday afternoon I went over to the suite to help pack it all up. Greer and the rest of the girls were already at it when I arrived, pulling the tacks out of Bri's Klimt poster and folding up her impressive collection of party clothes. "You guys are amazing," I said, watching as the five of them buzzed around the room with crisp, practiced efficiency.

Celine shrugged. "We take care of each other, right?" she asked, carefully wrapping a perfume bottle in a back issue of the *Crimson*. Then her chin wobbled. "At least, we fuckin' try."

"I . . . brought ice cream," I offered a little awkwardly, holding up the bag from the convenience store not far from Hemlock. "Is that weird?"

Keiko tilted her head. "I mean, kind of," she said, peering over and peeking inside the bag to see what flavors I'd picked. "But also, some might say, gentlemanly."

"Very gentlemanly," Greer echoed, shooting me a smile across the room. She grabbed a handful of stolen dining-hall spoons from the common-room kitchenette and we passed the pints around while we worked, emptying Bri's bureau and rolling up her little area rug, wrapping the cord of the desk lamp around its bendy gooseneck. "Thanks for coming," Greer murmured as I tucked Bri's schoolbooks into a banker's box, reaching over and laying one small hand on my back. "I'm really glad you're here."

"Yeah, of course," I said, goofily pleased in spite of everything, happy she was letting me help her in an actual, concrete way. I hadn't been able to figure out exactly how to be there for Greer the last few days. She'd slept in my room the last two nights, showing up late and crawling under my covers, though when I asked her she'd been adamant that she didn't want to talk. Once I'd woken up and she was crying. Once I'd woken up and she was gone. The university had offered her a bunch of different accommodations—time off, extended deadlines—and I was expecting her to jump at them, especially with how stressed she'd been about schoolwork. But she'd turned down every single one. "I just want everyone to treat me normally," she'd told me this morning over breakfast. "And that includes you."

It didn't take long for us to pack up the rest of Bri's things, her entire life at Harvard fitting neatly into a university-issued laundry cart. I thought about my mom, who'd lived in our apartment since before I was born and was woven inextricably into its every nook and crevice. I thought about how neatly I'd disappeared from Bartley after graduation, never to be heard from again.

I bent down to check under Bri's bed as we were finishing up, nudging a lacy thong out of the way with my sneaker as discreetly as possible before pulling out a broken hanger and a crumpled piece of college-ruled loose-leaf. I was about to toss the lot of it into the big black trash bag at the center of the room when I noticed a scrawl of red ink on the paper. I opened it as casually as I could, my eyes widening as I read the words:

Remember: you owe me.

Holy shit. I blinked, the words blurring and sharpening in front of my eyes like a Magic Eye. *You owe me.* Who the hell had written it? And what could Bri possibly owe? I thought again of the crushed-up pills on the desk the other morning. I thought again of the knocked-over lamp. I'd figured Bri had jostled it over herself as she fumbled clumsily toward Greer's mattress. But what if that wasn't what had happened at all?

"You okay?" Greer asked, glancing at me as she shut the door to the wardrobe.

I looked over at her half a beat too quickly, a familiar anxious restlessness growing in my body. It was the feeling of trying to work a blackberry seed out of a molar. It was the feeling of having a puzzle to solve. "Absolutely," I lied, then shoved the note in my pocket. "What's next?"

☙ ❧

Holiday took a ballet class on Wednesday evenings, but when I texted and told her it was an emergency she said I could pick her up when it was finished and we'd go get food at South Street Diner. I was waiting for her on Boylston Street when she came through the door with a scrum of other dancers at a little past nine, sweatpants pulled on over her leotard and her overflowing bag slung over one shoulder. "Hey!" she said, her face breaking open when she saw me.

"*Hey,*" agreed the tall, skinny guy in dance leggings walking beside her, raising his dark eyebrows suggestively. He turned to Holiday, his full mouth twisting. "Who's your boyfriend, Proctor?"

Holiday laughed. "Why," she asked, "is he handsome?" She shoved the guy playfully, then blew him and the rest of them a showy, exaggerated kiss. "He's not my boyfriend. I'll see you guys later, okay?"

"Handsome, huh?" I asked once we were alone on the sidewalk. "Is that what you'd call me?"

"Not to your face," Holiday shot back. "Come on." She nodded toward the corner. "I'm starving."

We turned onto Tremont and then again onto Stuart, walking south until we got to a grubby diner near the bus station. It had been a favorite of ours over the summer, in no small part because it stayed open all night long, and I breathed a weird, suprising sigh of relief as we slid into our usual booth at the back.

"So what's the big emergency?" she asked once we'd ordered, then ducked her head conspiratorially. "Are you pregnant? Because I'll take you to the clinic, Michael. I literally have Planned Parenthood saved in my phone for reproductive rights emergencies."

"Funny." I took a deep breath, my heart starting to beat a little bit harder; some part of me felt like I'd already wasted too much time. "You know that thing that happened on Martha's Vineyard a couple of summers ago?"

Holiday raised her eyebrows across the melamine table, her expression canny. *That thing that happened on Martha's Vineyard* was a body in a swimming pool; *that thing that happened on Martha's Vineyard* was a car chase. *That thing that happened on Martha's Vineyard* was the two of us screaming at each other in a pitch-black kitchen while a hurricane raged out the window and a murderer lurked on the other side of the door.

"Um, yeah" was all Holiday said, her thick eyebrows just barely twitching. "I think I remember it."

"What if I told you I think it might have happened again?"

I filled her in as quickly as possible on the events of the other morning, the pills and the EMTs and the cool gray pallor of Bri's skin against Greer's bright flowered sheets. "Holy shit," Holiday said when I was finished, her eyes wide and expressive behind her glasses. "Michael, that's *awful*. I heard a girl had OD'd over there, but I had no idea you were the one who found her. I'm so sorry. How's Greer doing? How are *you*?"

"I mean, I'm fine," I said, shrugging as manfully as possible. "And Greer is—you know. About how you'd expect her to be, considering her roommate just overdosed. Or at least, I *thought* she had overdosed? That's what I wanted to talk to you about. I was helping them all clear Bri's stuff out of the suite earlier this afternoon, and I found this under her bed."

I pulled the note out of my pocket and passed it across the table, watching as Holiday read its terse, all-caps contents. "That's . . . weird," she said finally, her warm fingers brushing mine as she handed it back.

"It is, right?" I nodded, gratified by her agreement. "It's totally weird."

"Could have been written by whoever she was buying from, conceivably."

"That's exactly what I was thinking," I said, pleased we were already on the same page. "And like, if she couldn't pay, maybe he killed her to send a message to his other clients."

Holiday frowned. "Whoa whoa whoa," she said, holding both hands up. "Hang on a second. I thought you said she overdosed."

"Well, yeah, that's what the EMTs seemed to think," I admitted. "But—"

"They would be the ones to know, right? And didn't you say she was like, a huge partier?"

"No, she definitely was," I allowed. "But there was also this lamp that got knocked over—"

"A lamp?"

"On the desk."

"Couldn't Bri have knocked it over herself before she passed out?"

"I mean, sure, I guess," I admitted, the slightest of edges creeping into my voice, "but—"

"Did they do an autopsy?"

"I have no idea," I said. "Maybe? I haven't like, heard anything about it. There was a bunch of crushed-up oxy on her desk, so I think they probably just assumed that's what she took."

"Were the police acting like they thought anything was suspicious?"

"I mean, they interviewed us."

"Harvard police?" she asked. "Or real police?"

"The Harvard police are real police."

"That's what it says on their website, yes," Holiday agreed with a wry smile. "What did they ask, stuff about Bri using?"

"About what happened that night," I recalled, "and when we found her. And yeah, about her being on drugs."

"Have they been back?"

"Well, no," I conceded, "but that doesn't mean anything, right?"

Holiday tilted her head like, *Not quite.* "Bri was a white girl in the Ivy League," she pointed out. "If there was even a whiff of something sketchy going on, they'd be all over it. Or forget the police, even—the *Herald* would be all over it. Or like, Fox 25."

I shrugged a little belligerently at that, sitting back against the ripped fake leather of the booth. It was a fucked-up assessment, but I couldn't act like it wasn't true. "I guess."

Both of us were quiet for a moment. Holiday took a long sip of her coffee. "Look," she said finally, her voice gentle, "I know first year is a mindfuck. Even if you think you're settling in fine, it's a lot to get used to. There's one girl on my floor who hasn't eaten anything but cereal since she got here. There's another one who makes her roommate leave the room every night between six and six-thirty so she can walk around naked for half an hour and air out all her various crevices."

I lifted an eyebrow. "Is it you?"

"Fuck off," Holiday said sweetly. "The point is, we're all still figuring out what we're doing here, even if we don't want to admit it. And what happened on the Vineyard last year was a thrill—I mean, a massively messed-up thrill, but still a thrill. It felt, like, purposeful. And concrete. I can get why you'd be looking for something like that now. But sometimes . . . an accident really is just an accident, you know? One weird note from a maybe-dealer does not a murder mystery make."

"Hold on a sec," I said, blinking at her across the table as I took in her meaning, my whole body flushed with humiliation and shame. "You think I'm manufacturing a violent crime because I'm *having trouble adjusting to college?*"

Right away, Holiday shook her head. "That's not what I'm—"

"Really?" I interrupted. "Because it kind of sounds like that's exactly what—"

"It's not," Holiday insisted. "Michael, come on. I just— Remember what I was saying the other day, about spending all your time with the lacrosse team? What if you joined a club, or something?"

"A *club*?" Oh, I was livid. I was so fucking pissed. "Screw you, Holiday. I bring something like this to you and you turn around and tell me I should join the literary magazine?"

Holiday blew a breath out. "Michael—" she started, then broke off as the waitress arrived and set our plates down, the smell of fried potatoes and bacon filling the air between us. We ate in silence for a moment, passing the ketchup sullenly back and forth. "Did you show it to Greer?" she asked me finally. "The note, I mean."

I shook my head, remembering the way Greer's body had crumpled to the floor the other night in the hallway. Remembering how she'd shaken in my arms. "She's like, super upset."

"I mean, understandably," Holiday pointed out. "I'm sure everyone is. It's an upsetting thing." She sighed. "I don't want to fight with you, okay? I felt like we were kind of fighting the other day by the river too. But you're my best friend. I'm so happy we're living in the same place again. And I'm really sorry this whole thing happened. Also," she said, bumping my ankle with hers underneath the table, "just saying, if you want to hang out with me so bad, you don't need to bring me a murder investigation to work on. All you need to do is say so."

I rolled my eyes. "Fuck off," I said, but I was smiling, I couldn't help it. I reached over and snagged a fry off her plate.

We ate our greasy food and drank our coffee and shot the shit for the better part of an hour, the knot in my chest loosening up just the slightest bit as Hall & Oates crooned from the speakers overhead. Holiday was right, probably. Her father taught criminology at Harvard; she had a bloodhound's nose for a mystery, and loved one more than anyone else I knew. She'd been the one to push us forward on the Vineyard, not to mention the one who'd ultimately cracked the whole thing wide open, and if she said there was nothing here to see, I knew it wasn't because she wasn't interested. It was because there was nothing here to see.

So why couldn't I shake the feeling that something wasn't right?

It was almost midnight by the time I walked her back to her dorm, the night air damp on the back of my neck as a rat darted furtively under a car across the street. "You realize you don't have to do this," Holiday told me as we sidestepped a mountain range of black garbage bags oozing slime all over the curb. "I'm fine to get back on my own."

I waved her off. "You and I both know my mom would cut my nuts off if she found out I let you walk home by yourself this late," I reminded her. It was factually correct, maybe, but it was also the truth that I didn't want to say goodnight to her just yet. We'd spent all summer breathing each other's air, eating butter and jam bagels from Forge and playing Scrabble on her parents' back patio; I forgot sometimes, when I didn't see her for a while, how much better things were when I did.

"So here's a question," Holiday said as we rounded the corner, the marquee of the Colonial winking cheerfully down the block. "Are you around the Friday before Thanksgiving? I'm in a showcase here, a musical theater thing down in the cabaret in my building. I'm singing a song from *Bridges of Madison County.*"

"Isn't that a movie?" I asked.

"It's a musical too," she explained. "It only ran for a few months on Broadway; the music is beautiful but not terribly commercial, and in the current theater climate— Anyway." She shook her head. "I'm the only first year they picked, so."

"Seriously?" I raised my eyebrows. "That's awesome, Holiday."

"It's not a big deal," Holiday said with a shrug. "But if you're around, you should come. Assuming of course that you can take some time away from your jam-packed schedule of goldfish eating."

I winced. "You heard about that too, huh?"

"I may have."

"Well," I said, rubbing at my neck as we slowed to a stop at the entrance to her building. "I'm busy, but I'm not that busy. I'll definitely be there."

"Okay," she said with a smile. "It's a date."

I said my goodnights, then looked both ways before crossing the street in the direction of the T stop. I'd almost reached the entrance when she called out. "Hey, Michael!" she hollered, her voice loud in the late-night quiet. "Murder or not: I'm glad you texted."

I grinned at her in the green glow of the traffic light, then turned and headed down into the dark mouth of the tunnel. Murder or not, I was glad I had too.

7

Thursday, 10/31/24-Friday, 11/1/24

GREER INVITED ME OVER TO THE SUITE TO PREGAME
Bri's memorial service.

"To *what*, now?" I asked, laughing a little nervously. We were
walking across campus, the sun setting above the science buildings; I'd picked her up from her last class of the day. It was Halloween, though neither of us was feeling particularly festive. The
air smelled like woodsmoke and leaves.

"You heard me." She shrugged, lips twisting. For the first time
since Bri died, there was a little spark of mischief in her expression.
"We decided it's what she would have liked."

It *was* undeniably on-brand, as far as tributes went; still: "You
sure you want me there?" I asked. "I get if you guys want to have,
like, girl time."

Greer nodded. "You showed up for me in a big way this week,
Linden. For the whole suite, really, but especially for me." She
reached over and took my hand, lacing our fingers together. "Like
it or not, you're in it now. You're one of us."

"Richard Gere pregame for life," I joked.

"Exactly."

We followed the winding path back toward Hemlock, passing a group of girls made up like the Kardashians and a cluster of grad students dressed as DNA. The Grim Reaper scuttled silently up behind us, scythe held like a flag in the air, and I shuddered before I could quell the impulse. I'd been expecting to feel less rattled after my conversation with Holiday—if she said I was reaching, then I was reaching, end of story—but instead, I'd spent the whole day turning that note over in my head, reading it again and again until the paper had gone soft and damp in my hands. I couldn't shake the notion that something wasn't right, that there was something about Bri's death that I wasn't seeing clearly.

I was obsessing, that was all. I needed to let it go.

The service was scheduled for noon on Friday. I went over to the suite around eleven and found the five of them clustered on the couch in the common room, passing a bottle of Fireball back and forth. "We started without you," Margot informed me, holding her shot glass up in a salute.

I nodded seriously. "I see that."

I watched as Dagny poured a shot of cinnamon whiskey into a coffee mug, then handed it over to me before raising the bottle. "To Bri," she said, waving it with a little flourish. "We miss you, you wild bird."

"You bright light," Greer added.

"You crazy bitch," Margot put in.

I smiled as all five of them busted up laughing. "To Bri," we all echoed, and drank. I winced at the familiar burn of the Fireball, then nodded at this morning's issue of the *Crimson,* which was lying wrinkled on the coffee table.

"Is the stuff about Bri as bad as you thought it was going to be?" I asked Dagny.

"Worse," Greer answered instead, flopping backward onto the sofa and plopping her feet into Celine's lap. "I am actually completely beside myself over the way everyone is talking about her."

"I know," Celine agreed, squeezing Greer's toes through her bright, fuzzy socks. "It sucks."

"How are people talking about her?" I asked.

"Don't act like you haven't heard them," Greer said, eyeing me from her still-prone position.

"I haven't," I said, which was a lie—of course I had, but I wanted to hear her say it. "I'm not the kind of guy people gossip to."

"Oh, please." Margot rolled her eyes.

"No, he's right, actually," Greer said with a small smile. "He's not. It's because his face is so punchable. It makes him hard to trust." Then, before I could dig into whatever the hell *that* meant, she continued: "You know how people are. Like, *Oh, it's so sad what happened,* but also, like, this fucked-up undertone of how she probably deserved it because she was a partier who liked to wear dresses that showed her underbutt. Which, she wasn't even that much of a partier, compared to a lot of the people in this school!"

I wasn't sure *that* was true—after all, Greer herself had complained about Bri's partying more than once, including the morning we found her. Still, it wasn't like I didn't take her point. There was a definite cautionary quality to the way people were talking about what had happened to Bri, an *isn't it awful but that's what you get* kind of smugness that made me a little uncomfortable. It was always surprising to me, the stories people told themselves about why someone else deserved whatever tragedies befell them. The stories of all the reasons they themselves would be safe.

"Nobody's actually saying anything mean about her, are they?" I asked, trying to sound casual. "Like, she didn't have any actual *enemies.*"

"Enemies?" Celine looked at me a little strangely, her expression reflected almost exactly in the other girls' faces. "No, of course not."

"Everybody loved Bri," Dagny said, "just like we did."

"No, totally," I said. "I guess I just meant—I don't know." I cringed a little. I was miserable at this kind of investigative work, interviewing people while trying to act like I wasn't. Not that I was interviewing anyone. Not that I was investigating. "Just like, nasty ex-boyfriends or whatever. People who might be spreading rumors on purpose."

"If anybody in this suite has a long list of jilted ex-lovers, it's Greer," Margot put in.

Greer huffed a laugh, her mouth dropping open. "Fuck off, Margot."

"Love you!" Margot sang in reply.

Greer rolled her eyes. "All right," she said, hauling herself up off the sofa. "Let's get ready for this shit show, shall we?"

"Greer," Dagny said, snorting, "Jesus."

"What?" Greer shot back. "You know as well as I do she would have hated this! Like, some nondenominational prayer service and all of us holding candles or whatever. It's a joke." She shook her head. "Now if you'll excuse me, I'm going to go dress in my mourning attire."

She stomped off down the hall, swaying a little from the Fireball. I stood there for a moment, unsure whether or not I was meant to follow.

"She's taking it really hard," Margot said after a moment, breaking the moody silence. "I mean, we all are, obviously, but it's worst for her."

"Yeah," I agreed quietly. "I can see that." I jammed my hands into my pockets. "I'll, uh. Let you guys get ready."

I headed down the hallway, knocking lightly on Greer's door before easing it open. She was prowling around the room in a bra and black tights, opening drawers and closing them again. I thought it was just nerves, or that she couldn't decide what to wear, but all at once she straightened up and turned to face me. "My watch is missing," she announced.

I frowned. "Your watch?"

"Well, my grandpa's watch. My grandma gave it to me when I got my acceptance letter here. It's a vintage Rolex, it's a whole—" She waved her hand. "Whatever, it's just going to make me sound douchey. Anyway, it was in my jewelry box, and now it's . . ." She opened the box one more time, then closed it again. "Not."

I glanced over my shoulder at the door. "Do you think whoever messed up your room took it?" In the chaos of everything that happened I'd never asked her whether it was actually Bri who'd been responsible that day, though judging by the look on her face now, I was pretty sure it hadn't been.

Sure enough, Greer shook her head. "I—maybe?" she admitted quietly. "I don't know. Hey, guys?" she called down the hallway toward the living room. "None of you have seen my watch lying around, have you?"

A chorus of "Nope" and "When was the last time you wore it" and "Did you check your nightstand, you know how you like to take off your jewelry when you drink" drifted down the hallway; something about their distraction, their lack of curiosity, made me wonder if possibly Greer hadn't told them her room had been trashed.

For her part, Greer only shrugged: "They're right," she said. "I probably just took it off somewhere and don't remember, that's all."

I nodded slowly. Personally, I couldn't imagine taking a vintage Rolex off somewhere and not remembering where I'd left it, but I didn't say that out loud. After all, it wasn't actually impossible that she'd lost it. I was used to stuff like this, the stark and sudden reminders between how people here had grown up and how I had. My roommate back at Bartley had once bet twenty-five hundred dollars on whether another kid on our hall could eat seven saltines in a minute; when it turned out he couldn't, Jasper only shrugged and dug the cash out of a box on his bookshelf, joking about how he hoped his weed dealer took cards.

Now I sat on the bed, watching as Greer looked half-heartedly around the room for a while longer before finally giving up and scooping a simple black dress off the back of the desk chair, tugging it over her head. "I don't know," she conceded, climbing onto the mattress and putting her head in my lap. "It's gone. Add it to the long list of reasons for my parents to be disappointed in me, I guess."

"Will do," I promised, smoothing her hair back off her forehead. "Is there like an Excel document somewhere?"

"They keep it in Google Sheets," she replied, rolling over to look up at me. "That way it's easily sharable."

"Sounds efficient."

"They are that."

We were quiet for a moment, both of us thinking. "Can I ask you something?" I ventured, unable to help myself. "What did Margot mean out there? About all your jilted ex-lovers?"

Greer snorted in disbelief at that, reaching up and pressing the heels of her hands into her eye sockets. "Oh, Linden," she said, "please don't."

"I'm not," I said quickly, holding my hands up. "I'm not."

"It's literally the day of my best friend's memorial service."

"No, I know." I winced. "I'm sorry. That was douchey."

Greer sighed, dropping her hands from her face. She looked exhausted. "It's fine," she said, shaking her head a little, like she was too worn out to argue. "I basically asked you the same thing the other day, didn't I? About all the girls you hooked up with?"

It felt like a million years ago already, the cold, sunny afternoon we'd gone to Castle Island. Still: "Yeah," I admitted. "I guess you kind of did."

We gazed at each other for a moment. I could see the flecks of gold in her eyes. It wasn't the right time, probably; I could easily see a universe where it was never the right time, where we hovered in this in-between until graduation, so I took a deep breath, then bent down and pressed my mouth gently against hers. "I've wanted to do that since I got to campus," I confessed quietly.

"I know." Greer grinned.

I wrinkled my nose. "That obvious?"

"A little obvious," she said, boosting herself upright. "But that's fine. I wanted it too."

"You did?"

"I did," Greer said, and lifted her face to mine.

"Hey, Greer, honey?" Margot asked, knocking on the door at the same time as she opened it, Greer and I pulling quickly apart. "We gotta get going."

Greer nodded. "Yeah," she said. "We'll be right out."

"Okay," Margot agreed. She looked back and forth between us for a moment, a small smile playing over her catlike features. "For the record," she said, turning and calling over her shoulder, "Bri would have liked that too."

∂∿℃

Bri's service was at MemChurch, the Memorial Church of Harvard University, a tall, airy space full of glossy wooden pews and polished marble columns. Sunlight streamed through the arched leaded windows. The crimson carpet up the aisle seemed to glow.

Greer was almost finished with her reading, a poem by Ada Limón, when my phone buzzed with a text. I ignored it, but a second later it buzzed again, then started humming with the insistent swarm that meant someone was calling. I pulled the thing out of my pocket, snuck a look at the screen: Holiday.

Not a good time, I texted as furtively as I could.

She texted back barely a second later: *It's important.*

I sighed and edged toward the aisle, earning dirty looks from both Dagny and Margot for my trouble, then made my way to the back and out the heavy door of the chapel. "Dude," I said when she answered, ducking into the stairwell that led to the choir loft, "I'm literally in the middle of Bri's memorial service."

"Seriously?" Holiday sounded incredulous. "What the hell are you doing calling me?"

"You said it was important!"

"I mean, it could have waited until—whatever," Holiday said impatiently. "Okay. Well. While I have you. You said there was a bunch of crushed-up oxy on the desk when you found Bri, right?"

"Yeah," I recalled slowly. "Why?"

"I felt kind of bad about blowing you off at the diner the other night," she explained. "So I called a friend at the medical examiner's office—"

"Hang on," I interrupted. "You have a friend at the medical examiner's office?"

Holiday sighed, like she had suspected she'd need to explain this part but had hoped I'd know enough to just accept and move on. "We met in After Hours fandom," she informed me, naming the boy band she'd been obsessed with since middle school. "She writes, like, the raunchiest fan fiction you've ever read in your life."

"And she's the *medical* examiner?"

"Did I *say* she was the medical examiner?" Holiday countered. "She just works there. She does IT or something. Don't be ridiculous."

"Oh, *I'm* the one being ridiculous."

"The point is," Holiday pressed on, "she told me that it's regular procedure for them to do an autopsy on all drug overdose cases, even if the deaths aren't being investigated as suspicious. And according to the records she pulled up for me, Bri's official cause of death *is* an overdose—but all they found in her system besides alcohol was Adderall and Molly."

I frowned. "Not oxy?"

"Not oxy."

"But if there was no oxy in her system—"

"Then what was the oxy doing on the desk?" she asked. "Yeah, I don't know."

I sat down hard on the landing, weirdly vindicated and a little afraid. "So the cops must be investigating, then."

"I don't actually think so," Holiday admitted, her voice low and urgent. "She said it doesn't look like the Cambridge PD has requested the autopsy report." Then, before I could respond: "There's one more thing. I did a little bit of research, and like, obviously I'm *also* not the medical examiner, but from what I read, if they're just running a basic toxicology panel to confirm there were drugs in her system, it's possible they weren't necessarily looking for another cause of death."

I frowned. "Meaning—"

"Meaning it's possible—probable, even—that Bri drank a lot, took a bunch of drugs, knocked over a lamp, passed out in Greer's bed, and never woke up," Holiday reminded me, "and that's a tragedy. But it's *also* possible she drank a lot and took a bunch of drugs—"

"And then somebody smothered her with a pillow and left

different drugs on the desk to point the cops in the wrong direction and nobody caught it?"

"Well," Holiday pointed out, "not *nobody*."

Downstairs in the chapel the service was wrapping up, a hundred voices rising and falling together as the pianist played a plinky rendition of "Somewhere Over the Rainbow." Sunlight trickled through a window at the top of the staircase, a million motes of dust hovering in the air. "No," I agreed slowly, rubbed a hand over my forehead as I stood on wobbly legs to face whatever was about to happen. "Not nobody."

8

Saturday, 11/2/24-Monday, 11/4/24

MY MOM CALLED FIRST THING THE FOLLOWING MORN-
ing. "I'm downstairs," she said brightly. "Outside your building. I
thought I could take you to breakfast."

"Oh! Um." I sat up, looking around wildly. I wasn't *in* my
building, was the first problem that presented itself. I was in
Greer's building. More specifically, I was in Greer's *bed*—well, Bri's
bed, technically, which Greer had taken to sleeping in. "I, um. I
have class?"

I realized a beat too late that it was Saturday, but my mom was
already laughing, the sound of it warm and familiar on the other
end of the phone. "I'm kidding, sweetheart," she promised, "but
your horrified voice is something that will stay with me long into
the future, so thank you for that."

"I'm not *horrified*," I protested, feeling a little ashamed of myself. "I just—"

"Don't relish the idea of your mother showing up unannounced outside your college dorm?" she asked. "I suppose you can be forgiven."

"Thank you."

We talked for a little while, catching up on the hygiene kits she was putting together for her mutual aid group and the hike in the White Mountains she was doing with her dorky boyfriend Paul. She'd been calling more frequently since I'd told her about Bri, I'd noticed, making cheerful conversation while probing carefully around the edges of my life, looking for snags in the fabric. "How are you doing?" she asked me finally. "You doing okay?"

I glanced at Greer, still asleep with one elegant arm slung over her face. I thought of Holiday's voice yesterday on the phone. I remembered the meeting I still hadn't scheduled with Professor McMorrow, knowing even as I made a mental note to do it sometime this week that I probably wasn't going to. "I am," I promised quietly. "I'm doing okay."

"Holiday says you're back with your girlfriend."

"Okay," I said, squeezing my eyes shut. "Very nice. Goodbye, Mother!"

"I'm just asking!" she insisted, her laugh high and musical. She was still chuckling to herself when I hung up the phone.

Holiday was visiting friends at NYU for the weekend, which meant three full days before we could meet to make a game plan for investigating whatever had happened to Bri. "You don't want

82

to skip your trip, do you?" I'd asked hopefully; when the question was met only with withering silence on the other end of the phone, I winced. "Not skipping it!" I amended. "Enough said."

I spent the weekend trying to distract myself, going for my usual Saturday run along the river and meeting with my group for a project in Race, Gender, and Performance. Coach had scheduled an all-team workout on Sunday afternoon—lacrosse was a spring sport, technically, but we met at the gym three times a week all through the fall, building muscle and endurance and, ostensibly, team spirit, though that last part was something of a going concern.

I changed my clothes in the locker room, nodding at my teammates as I took my place on the treadmill and jammed my headphones into my ears. Something felt strange, though, and it took me a moment to figure out what it was: the *quiet*, I realized belatedly, a palpable peace that had been missing all semester long. Nobody slapping me a little too hard between the shoulder blades. Nobody threatening to make me eat a turtle. "Where's Hunter?" I asked, yanking out an earbud.

"Dude," Cam said from the treadmill beside me. "You didn't hear? He's suspended."

I blinked, breaking my stride and almost losing my footing. "From school?"

Cam shook his head. "Just from practice, I think. He beat the shit out of that kid Oliver for being too mouthy."

"Seriously?" That startled me; Hunter was a douchebag and a bully, absolutely, but to hurt someone so badly he risked his place on the team?

"It was a whole thing," Cam continued, still sprinting merrily along on the neighboring treadmill. "Oliver wasn't going to rat him out or anything, but Hunter knocked his tooth out and Coach didn't buy his story about falling out of his bunk bed." He shook his head. "I don't know. Hunter's always been a dick, but it feels like he's getting worse lately. Your girl Greer was right to dump him when she did."

I fell right the fuck off the treadmill. "I'm sorry," I said, sprawled on my ass on the industrial carpet, "*what?*"

Right away, Cam looked like he wished a giant eagle would swoop down from the sky and carry him off into the ether, never to be heard from again. "Oh, fuck me," he said. "Dude, are you okay?" He winced. "Bro, I thought you knew."

"I did . . . not know," I clarified, getting clumsily to my feet.

"Clearly," Cam said, rubbing a hand over his face. "I see that now. But, dude, how did Hunter not say anything? Like, the guy is not exactly what one might call subtle. I would have bet money that at some point he'd been like, *Yo, Linden, just FYI, I spent most of last year giving your ex the busine—*"

"Enough," I interrupted, more loudly than I meant to. Obviously, Greer and I had been apart last year. Of course I knew intellectually that she didn't owe me anything, that she was allowed to date whoever she wanted. I could have recited Holiday's lecture myself.

Still, though: *Hunter?*

"Dude," Cam tried now, "I didn't mean to—"

But I waved him off, getting back on the treadmill and punching the speed up as high as it would go. "Don't worry about it," I said. "Let's just get through this, all right?"

"Sure, bro," Cam said. "Let's just get through it."

❧

I found Greer on the third floor of the library. For a person who, in all honesty, had never been much of a reader, I'd loved the Widener since the moment I'd first stepped onto Harvard's campus: the grand marble staircases and the intricate Greek columns, the soaring murals by John Singer Sargent and the study lamps shaded with glass. It felt like the kind of place you could conceivably find a portal to another dimension. It felt like the kind of place you might go to think deep thoughts.

"You and Hunter used to *date*?" I asked when I spotted her sitting at a carrel in the corner, a big plaid scarf wrapped around her like a blanket as she squinted at a dense-looking bio textbook, her hair in a thick, glossy braid over one shoulder.

For a moment Greer just looked at me. Then, very calmly, she closed her book and set down her highlighter. "Hello to you too."

"How could you not have told me that?" I asked, trying not to sound as wounded as I felt. I didn't want to act like a girl about this, but shit. "This whole time."

Greer pushed her chair back, turning to face me. "First of all," she said, using one finger to draw an imaginary circle around my person, "did you even bother to shower before you came over here to show your sweaty ass to everyone on campus?" She wrinkled her nose underneath her glasses. "Second of all, I'm allowed to not tell you things, Linden. The two of us hanging out again doesn't automatically entitle you to all of me."

"I'm not saying it does!" I argued, loudly enough that a girl at a neighboring carrel looked up from her laptop and shot me an exquisitely dirty look. "All I'm saying is that it would have been nice to know, when Hunter was making my life a living hell for the last two months, that it wasn't actually personal."

"Of course it was personal." Greer rolled her eyes. "Did you somehow miss the memo about your extremely punchable face?"

I didn't laugh. "Is this not a big deal to you?" I asked. "You and me? Because I gotta tell you, Greer, maybe it's not cool of me to say or whatever, but it's a big deal to me. *You're* a big deal to me." I scrubbed a hand over the back of my head. "You always have been."

Greer gazed at me for another long moment. Then she sighed. "We were together for like twenty minutes last spring," she told me. "I don't even think it was exclusive, on his part. I broke it off before finals for like . . . obvious reasons—"

"He can't read?" I supplied dryly.

Greer's expression was supremely unimpressed. "He . . . does not have a rich inner life," she continued, as if I hadn't spoken. "And he, like, did not take it great, so you'll have to forgive me if it's not the story I like to lead with when I'm talking to"—she waved a hand in my general direction—"potential suitors."

That stopped me, the skin on my lower back prickling as I thought about Oliver's busted tooth. All at once, I forgot I was pissed. "What do you mean, he didn't take it great?"

Greer shrugged inside her sweatshirt, tugging the scarf more tightly around her. "You've met him," she said, like that should have been enough of an explanation. "It wasn't a big deal. He just said a bunch of nasty stuff, that's all. Left a couple of choice comments on my Instagram. Real charmer." Greer sighed then, holding her hands out like, *What do you want from me?* "In case it wasn't abundantly clear, Linden, I'm already not having the best week of my entire life. And I have to study if I don't want to wind up commuting to Western Connecticut State University for spring semester, so." Her eyes filled with tears behind her glasses. "Fuck off, okay?"

Right away, I felt like the biggest asshole who'd ever lived. "I'm sorry," I said, reaching for her—pulling her out of her chair and wrapping my arms around her, ignoring the exaggerated sigh of Irritated Laptop Girl one carrel over. "I'm sorry. I'm sorry. I'm being a weirdo."

"You *really* are," Greer agreed, but she let me hold her—her body deflating a little as she wrapped her arms around my neck and hung there for a moment, letting me take her weight. "It sucked, okay?" she mumbled into my chest, her voice muffled against my hoodie. "The whole thing with Hunter."

"I hear you," I said quietly. "We don't have to—I mean, your business is your business. I didn't mean to, like, pry."

"Thank you," she said—or that was what it sounded like, anyway; I was momentarily distracted by Laptop Girl slamming her computer shut and huffing off into the dimly lit stacks. "I appreciate that."

"I gotta say, though," I ventured, smoothing my palms over the warm cotton of Greer's sweatshirt, breathing in her cherry Chap-Stick smell, "I don't really think I qualify as a *potential* suitor at this point."

Greer snorted. "Oh no?" she asked, pulling back and tilting her face up to look at me. "Then what are you, exactly?"

I shrugged inside her arms. "You tell me."

Greer seemed to consider that. For a second it seemed like she might be about to soften; for a second it even seemed like she might be about to kiss me, but in the end she just smiled and ducked neatly out of my grip. "I don't think I will," she said sweetly, then turned to collect her textbooks, sliding her stuff back into her bag. "Come on," she said, slinging it over her shoulder and lacing her fingers through mine, tugging me toward the staircase. "Let's go get something to eat."

9

Thursday, 11/7/24

"IT'S NOT THAT I'M *JEALOUS*," I INSISTED ON THURSDAY, slurping dejectedly at an iced coffee even though the temperature was close to freezing. "I mean, Hunter can barely walk upright. He thinks Audre Lorde is a flavor of Muscle Milk. I'm not *intimidated* by him. I just don't get why Greer wouldn't have mentioned it, you know? Like, if it's really over, if it really wasn't a big deal, then why wouldn't she have just said— Are you listening?"

"Nope!" Holiday said brightly. It had taken almost the whole week to find a time we could meet, and we'd finally caught up at a coffee shop in Central, a hipster place with mismatched mugs and the kind of ratty, sagging couches that always made me worry I was going to pick up bedbugs. Holiday had no such qualms, apparently, dropping herself down onto the cushions with such abandon that her cup overflowed, its weedy-smelling contents sloshing down onto her arm and into the sleeve of her sweater. It looked hand-knit, gray with a bunch of tiny white pom-poms on it. "Although I can't help but observe that for a person who was so anxious to get to crime-solvin' he wanted me to give up my very expensive theater tickets last weekend, you seem to be having an awfully hard time focusing."

"Fair enough," I admitted, stuffing a bite of scone into my mouth. "Let's get started."

Holiday nodded briskly. "Let's." She bent down and pulled her notebook out of her bag, a thick, wide-ruled tome with her name embossed in gold on the cover. She'd had some variation on that notebook as long as I'd known her; she'd probably been the only elementary schooler in Cambridge with a monogrammed assignment pad from FranklinCovey. She always wrote in bright purple pen. "What do we know about Bri?"

"Not a ton," I confessed, parroting back the stuff she'd told me in the living room of the lax house the night of the party, the slivers of knowledge I'd gleaned from Greer. I thought back to the last time Holiday and I had done this, sitting across from each other in a coffee shop on Martha's Vineyard. Our suspect list then had been enormous—our victim had gone through life as if he was trying specifically to piss people off whenever possible. But Bri hadn't been like that. Judging from the remembrances of her in the *Crimson*—to hear Greer and Dagny talk about it, you'd have thought it was a total hit job, but actually most of it was quite nice and sincere—most people had liked her a lot. "I think we should probably start by trying to find her dealer," I concluded finally. "Somebody in the suite will know who it was, I'm pretty sure. All six of them were like, super close."

"Are you sure?" Holiday asked. "How much time have you spent in that suite?"

"A good amount," I defended myself. "And it isn't some, like, *Mean Girls* thing. They're all best friends."

"I'm not saying they're mean girls," Holiday countered, in a voice like she was making fun of me a little but hoping I wouldn't notice. "But everyone has enemies."

"Even you?"

"Well, no, not *me*," Holiday admitted, batting her eyelashes across the coffee table. "Everybody likes me. But I'm a special case."

"You're something," I muttered. "I will give you that much."

Holiday had me pull up Bri's social media accounts, which had already turned into morbid digital memorials, and we scrolled back as far as we could before working our way forward again: Bri in high school with her softball team, Bri experimenting with blond highlights at the prom. Most of the pictures from the last year or so were of her with the girls from the suite: Bri and Dagny apple picking, Bri and Keiko and Celine dressed up for freshman formal. All six of them mugging in front of Hemlock House on move-in day this past August.

"They look like sisters," Holiday observed, peering over my shoulder. She'd settled herself onto the couch beside me so we could look at the phone together, a lock of her hair brushing the side of my cheek. "Bri and Greer, I mean."

"Yeah," I agreed. "They kind of do." I hadn't paid that much attention to it before, but all at once I couldn't unsee it: the hair and eyes, sure, but also the way they held themselves. Even their bone structure was kind of similar.

"Hang on," Holiday said, batting my hand out of the way to look at the picture more closely, then straightening up and turning to face me. "You said Bri was in Greer's bed when you found her, right?"

"Yeah." I frowned. "Why?"

"And she was wearing Greer's clothes." She took the phone from my hand and scrolled back to the last photo in Bri's feed—maybe the last photo of her, period. "That green tank top, right? You said it was Greer's?"

"Yeah," I said again. "I mean, they shared clothes a lot, I think."

"And the note—" She reached for it, pulling it across the table to look at it one more time. "It doesn't have Bri's name on it specifically."

"No," I said, beginning to understand what Holiday was driving at. "Oh, *shit,* Holiday."

Holiday nodded, her dark eyes shining. "They look sort of similar, right? Like, if, say, Bri got drunk at that party, came home, and passed out in the bed that was closer to the door. And then someone came in looking for Greer, saw a brunette passed out in her bed?"

"Yeah," I said. It felt like I was looking through a kaleidoscope, turning it so that all the colored glass shifted inside and made an entirely new picture. "It's definitely possible."

"Okay." Holiday flipped to a new page in her notebook as I reached absently for the last of the scone. "In that case: Who would want to hurt *Greer*?"

I thought again of Greer's trashed bedroom. I thought of Hunter getting suspended from the team.

"Holiday," I said, the last of the scone sticking in my throat as I swallowed. "Hear me out."

We ordered another round of drinks and I laid it all out for her as coherently as I could manage, Greer's missing watch and Hunter's nasty Instagram comments and Oliver Beckett's broken tooth. "I don't know," Holiday said slowly. "If Greer and Hunter dated, what are the odds of him mistaking Bri for Greer?"

"If he was shit-faced and pissed off and nursing a grudge?" I countered. "And she was already asleep in Greer's bed?"

"Beer goggles meets confirmation bias," Holiday mused. "Sure, I'll buy it."

"It's not a bad theory, is it?" I pressed, cringing a little when I heard how eager I sounded for her approval. "Hunter used to date Greer and was mad she broke up with him. That's motive. He's a big, jacked, douchey lacrosse player. That's means. And—" I paused, frowning a little. "Wait, what's the third thing?"

"Opportunity," Holiday reminded me, licking tea off the inside of her wrist.

"Opportunity!" I agreed. "Which, actually, now that I think about it—Hunter left the party before me the night that Bri died, which is weird on account of he literally lives in the lax house. Like, where was he going, if not over to Hemlock?"

"Twenty-four-hour CVS," Holiday guessed immediately, ticking the options off on her fingers. "The bar at the Hong Kong. All-night hot dog buffet truck on Revere Beach Parkway."

"I'm serious!" I said, kicking her lightly in the combat boot. "I do miss that hot dog truck, though."

"Same," Holiday agreed; we'd been regulars over the summer, loading up our hot dogs with chili and hot peppers and eating them while we listened to horror podcasts in her car. She held her hand out, making grabby fingers in my direction. "Let me see what he looks like?"

She sat back on the mangy couch as I dug my phone out of my pocket, her hands wrapped tight around her London Fog. "It *is* a good theory," she mused, "but a good theory isn't enough. We need to put Hunter in Hemlock House the night Bri died."

"How?" I asked distractedly, clicking through the app until I found Hunter's profile.

"I don't know yet." Holiday shrugged into the cushions. "What about the note?" she asked. " 'You owe me'? Like, what would Greer owe to Hunter? I guess sex, conceivably, in his opinion, but—"

"Here he is," I interrupted, not particularly wanting to follow the thread of that inquiry. I passed her the phone. "Hunter Hayes."

Holiday snorted a laugh. "That's not his real name," she said immediately. "That's the name of someone who cheats in a sailboat regatta in an episode of a WB show from the early aughts."

"First of all, I don't know that *you're* exactly in a position to talk about whose name does or doesn't sound real," I teased. "Second of all, how would you cheat in a sailboat regatta?"

Holiday eyed me darkly. "There are ways."

"I'll take your word for it."

She flicked idly through Hunter's profile for a moment, then handed the phone back to me. "What's the security situation at

Harvard?" she asked. "You can't use your ID card to get into a building you don't live in, can you?"

I shook my head. "No, but people let each other in all the time. That wouldn't have stopped him."

"No security desk?" she pressed hopefully. "Nobody who might have seen him come in that night?"

I shook my head. "Harvard uses a private security company in a lot of their buildings, to handle lockouts for first-years and garden-variety stuff like that," I explained. "Some of the houses—including mine, actually—do have a main desk, but Hemlock isn't one of them."

"Of course it isn't." Holiday sighed.

"There are cameras, though," I offered. "I don't know if there's one near the front door of that building, but if I had to guess—"

Holiday brightened. "Okay," she said, "that's definitely something to check out, then. And do you want to try to see what you can find out from Greer's suitemates, meanwhile? If Hunter has been giving her a hard time lately, they'll be the ones to know it." She took a sip of her latte. "Unless you want to talk to her about it directly?"

"And tell her you and I are working on a theory that Hunter was trying to kill her but missed, even though we have absolutely no evidence to back it up?" I asked. "Not particularly, no."

"Fair," Holiday admitted. "Even I would probably have a hard time selling that one."

"Only probably?"

"I'm very convincing," she said with a shrug. "But you're right that it makes most sense at this point if we don't loop her in." She was quiet for a moment, thinking. I could almost see the synapses firing behind her eyes, exploding like the fireworks over the Charles every Fourth of July. "Not yet, anyway."

৯৩

Holiday wanted to see Hemlock House for herself, so we finished our drinks and she walked me back to campus, our feet crunching the dry, brittle leaves. We'd changed the clocks back this weekend, winter barreling down the tracks in our direction like an Acela made of sleet and hail. We passed the wide stone steps that led to Hemlock's main entrance—"Bingo," Holiday murmured, nodding at a security camera mounted on one of the columns—then looped through the courtyard and back past the dumpsters behind the building. "Really getting your money's worth from that private security company, huh?" she asked, smirking at the unmistakable fug of weed smoke drifting out of the alley. Some of the guards liked to take their breaks back there, in particular a couple of skinny white dudes who couldn't have been much older than us; I'd seen them shuffling smilingly back to their posts a couple of times, their eyes gone a telltale red.

"Yeah," I agreed, "it's a full Paul Blart situation. I actually kind of don't blame Greer for not wanting to go to them about her watch."

"She didn't report it?" Holiday asked curiously.

"No, no, she did in the end," I said, "but they were basically like, *Cool, we'll keep an eye out, have you checked the lost and found?*"

Holiday hummed quietly, glancing behind her at the alley one more time before pulling her phone out of her coat pocket and scowling at the clock. "I gotta get across the river," she reported. "I have a rehearsal tonight."

"What about Hunter?" I asked before I could stop myself.

"I think he mostly rehearses in the morning," she deadpanned, then made a face at me. "Goodbye, Michael!"

☜☞

I brought a box of cookies from Flour over to Hemlock that night, partly because it felt like a nice thing to do for a group of girls who had recently lost a suitemate and partly because I wanted to see if I could find out anything else about Hunter but wasn't one hundred percent sure Greer was done being mad at me, so thought it was best to buy her forgiveness and trust with expensive baked goods. Four of the five of them were camped out in the common room when I knocked on the open door of the suite, Keiko doodling on her iPad while Greer bent over her sociology homework at the breakfast bar. Margot and Dagny were playing gin rummy on the wobbly university-issued coffee table.

"Linden," Dagny greeted me; her voice was the one you might use to say hello to the annoying neighbor on a TV sitcom from the '90s, which was how I knew Greer had told them what I'd said to her back at the library. "You're looking well."

"Uh, thanks," I said, lifting the bakery box. "I brought dessert."

"That's what I like to hear," Keiko said, holding a hand out without bothering to look up from her screen.

I passed it over, bumping my shoulder against Greer's. "Hi," I said softly.

She lifted an eyebrow, noncommittal. "Hi yourself."

"Anyway," Margot said, picking up the thread of a conversation that had obviously been in progress before I got there, "my bitchy aunt Jane is using the house to host actual dinner on the Thursday, but they're all going to clear out on Friday morning and go to Stratton for the weekend if you guys want to drive up that night."

"We're going to Margot's family's camp the weekend after Thanksgiving," Greer informed me.

"You should come with," Margot offered. "My cousin and a couple of his buddies are going to be there, and Celine's bringing her pervert boyfriend from Bowdoin, so. Really it's a free-for-all."

"Fuck you!" Celine called from inside her bedroom, her voice muffled through the door. "He's not a pervert."

"Of course he's not!" Margot called back, then rolled her eyes. "Full pervert," she assured me, dropping her voice a little. "He literally asked her to send him a picture of her—"

"I'd love to," I interrupted quickly. "Come to the camp, I mean. Assuming Greer wants me there."

"I think I can probably tolerate you," Greer said thoughtfully, biting into a ginger molasses cookie. "Assuming you bring more treats."

"Hey, dudes?" Celine asked before I could answer, padding

barefoot into the common room in her bathrobe. "Have any of you seen a necklace floating around in the bathroom or anywhere? That Georgette McKeown one I have, the rose gold *C*?"

I watched as the rest of the girls shook their heads. "That reminds me," Keiko said, twisting around on the sofa to look at Greer, "did you ever find your watch?"

"I sure did not," Greer said, "though to be clear, if my dad asks, it's safe and sound and you all saw me wear it to class the other day, where I delivered half a dozen clever answers and aced a pop quiz."

"A stunning performance," Keiko agreed seriously. "You were truly a shining star."

"You know," Dagny put in, her dark brow creasing as she pulled one leg up underneath her on the sofa, "Phoebe Chung on the third floor was saying she had a ring go missing the other day. I wonder if there's, like—"

"A Hemlock House bandit?" Margot asked with a laugh. "Creeping through the suites in a striped shirt and skullcap like the Hamburglar?"

"I mean, it kind of feels that way, doesn't it?" Dagny asked. "It seems weird that like, all of you guys would suddenly lose your shit at the same time."

Greer caught my eye across the common room. "Remember the underwear thief back at Bartley?" she asked with a grin.

"Woe unto you who leaves his dryer unattended, et cetera," I said, but the truth is, I wasn't really listening. My mind was racing—the possibilities unfurling in a million different directions, the threads unspooling too quickly for me to gather them up and stitch them back together into anything resembling a working theory. It had seemed plausible to me—likely, even—that Hunter might have taken Greer's watch as some kind of fucked-up trophy. But why would he have risked stealing from anyone else in Hemlock? Or were the thefts an entirely separate thing?

I ducked into the bathroom as the girls passed around the box of cookies, dug my phone out of my pocket. *Two more pieces of jewelry missing at Hemlock,* I texted Holiday quickly. *Celine in the suite and some girl on the third floor.*

Holiday texted back right away, a long string of exclamation points. *Okay,* she told me. *Well. A lot to think about THERE, clearly. But the good news is I think I might have an idea for how to get a look at that security footage.*

You do? I straightened up, a little thrill skittering through me. *How?*

Just walking into rehearsal, she wrote back. *More soon.*

10

Monday, 11/18/24

SOON TURNED OUT TO TAKE MORE THAN A WEEK, Holiday and I both busy with projects and papers, neither one of us with much time or energy to spare. Back on the Vineyard we'd had endless hours to devote to our amateur sleuthing, the days stretching out in front of us luxuriously empty. This time, we had to fit any investigative work into the margins of our actual lives: classes and practices, another reminder email from Professor McMorrow urging me tersely to make my advising appointment. Hunter returned to lacrosse workouts. The trees lost the rest of their leaves. The whole thing made me feel anxious and jangly, like with every passing day our case was growing colder. Like the longer we waited, the more time Hunter had to get away with whatever he'd done.

We finally managed to meet up the following Monday, Holiday taking the Red Line over to campus with the caveat that she had to get back for a rehearsal later that night. "Any luck with the suitemates?" she asked, checking the time on her phone before setting it down on the table between us. We were sitting in the coffee shop at the Smith Center, all white subway tile and marble-topped bistro tables. Jaunty, French-sounding jazz piped through a speaker overhead.

I shook my head. "Not really," I admitted. I'd given it my best shot at last week's Richard Gere pregame, waiting until Greer was in the bathroom and turning to Margot as casually as I could. "Can I ask you something?" I ventured, reaching for some popcorn in a way I hoped look natural and low-key. "I know Greer said Hunter gave her kind of a hard time when she broke up with him last year. He never made any, like, threats, did he?"

Margot looked at me a little strangely. Celine set down her phone. "No, not *threats*," Margot said. "Not really."

"Okay." I nodded, slinging an arm over the back of the sofa. "Do you have any reason to think Hunter would want to, like . . . hurt her?"

Oh, none of them liked that. Dagny's eyes widened; Keiko's mouth curled with distaste. "What the fuck, Linden?" Celine crossed her arms, leaning back away from me like whatever I had was catching. "That's a creepy fucking question to ask."

"No, I know," I said quickly. "I didn't mean it like—"

"What other ways are there to mean it?" Margot shook her head. "No. And also, from what Greer said, you were *also* kind of a little bitch when she ended things with you back at your boarding school. Did *you* want to hurt her?"

The toilet flushed just then, the bathroom door opening and Greer padding out into the common room. "Everything okay?" she asked.

"Well!" Holiday said now, her expression conveying a barely contained amusement. "I might have handled that a little bit differently, but I do as always admire your investigative chutzpah." She glanced at her phone one more time. "Anything they told you would have been circumstantial anyway, at least without hard evidence that Hunter was in Hemlock the night Bri died."

I nodded. "Speaking of which," I said, "what's the play for that, exactly? Just waltz into HUPD headquarters and bat your eyelashes until they agree to hand over the footage from the security cameras outside the building?"

"First of all, you say it like that exact technique hasn't worked extremely well for us before," Holiday reminded me archly. "Second of all, no. I've got a plan." She looked at her phone one more time, then popped the last bite of a chocolate croissant into her mouth, balling up her wax-paper bag and sliding down off her stool. "Come on," she said. "It's time."

ॐ

I followed Holiday back through campus, jogging a little to keep up. "If I did this right," she told me as we rounded the corner toward the rear of Hemlock House, "we should be able to catch these guys right . . . about . . . Yup."

I followed her gaze into the alley: sure enough, there were the same two security guards we'd seen the last time we'd been back here, a haze of smoke surrounding them like a cocoon.

"Hey!" Holiday called. They looked up in unison, twin joints held in their outstretched hands. "I really am sorry about this," she said, then held up her phone and snapped a picture.

"What the—" The taller one blanched. "Delete that!"

"I would love to," Holiday said sincerely, "and I will. I just need one quick favor from you guys first."

The guard's eyes narrowed. "What kind of favor?" he asked, suspicion written all over his pasty face.

Holiday grinned.

⁂

Ten minutes later I watched with some wonder as the taller guard—the last name on his badge said DiNapoli—used the key card looped on a Harvard University lanyard around his neck to unlock one of the small brick gatehouses that dotted campus, which the security guards who weren't assigned to specific buildings used as a home base when they weren't out on their rounds. "You better make this quick," the short one warned. "I mean it."

"In and out," Holiday promised seriously. "Nobody will even know we were here."

"Right," DiNapoli grumbled. "Sure they won't."

The shorter one scowled. "If we lose our jobs over this—"

"Respectfully," Holiday interrupted, holding up one finger, "if you lose your jobs over this, it will be because you couldn't wait to light up a J until you clocked out of your workplace for the evening, not because I caught you at it."

She sounded exactly like her mother—actually, she sounded exactly like *my* mother—in a way that made me laugh; I stifled the sound of it into a cough as best I could, though not before DiNapoli shot me a dirty look. We were not making any friends here today, that was for sure.

Holiday, for her part, didn't seem particularly worried about that. "We're looking for footage from one specific camera outside Hemlock House," she told him, nodding at the computer on the desktop. "From one specific date."

All four of us were silent for a moment as DiNapoli entered the appropriate values into the computer, Holiday sitting down at the desk to scroll through the results. I was peering over her shoulder when the shorter guard jabbed me in the side with one elbow. "Hey," he said, pointing at me accusingly. "Aren't you the kid who ate the goldfish?"

I winced even as Holiday snorted to herself, dragging the video footage along. "I didn't *eat* it," I tried, turning to frown at him. "I mean, I didn't, like, *chew*—"

"But you did in fact swallow a goldfish."

"I mean, technically."

"I don't see what's technical about it," the guard argued smugly. "You either swallowed a goldfish or you didn't."

"Okay," I said. "You know what, dude—"

"Shut up," Holiday said softly. "There he is. Hunter Hayes."

"Seriously?" I turned and looked back, as relieved for the interruption as I was excited she'd found him. I squinted at the screen, watching as Hunter strolled up the path and hopped up the last two steps, catching the door before it shut behind a guy who'd just keyed himself inside. Judging by the time stamp, he must have come directly here after I—*technically*—drank the goldfish.

The security guards watched as Holiday dutifully deleted the picture of them from her phone. "Off the cloud too," one of them prompted, and she nodded.

"Gentlemen," she said, holding a hand out. "Pleasure doing business with you." Neither one of them shook.

੓੓

"He was there," I said when we were alone again. It was hard not to feel pleased with myself—for once in our entire relationship, I'd been the one with the killer instincts. I'd known there was something off about Hunter this whole time, and this proved it. "It was him."

"That's our opportunity—" Holiday agreed.

"All three things!" I crowed.

"It's good," she admitted, "but it still isn't ironclad." She thought for a moment. "You guys have parties at the lacrosse house most weekends, right?"

"Looking to meet a nice guy?" I teased.

Holiday snorted. "I would truly rather renounce Judaism, join an order of nuns, and live out my days cloistered in an abbey singing hymns in Latin all night and day."

"Sounds peaceful."

"It does," she agreed, "but anyway, no. I want to get a look inside Hunter's bedroom."

"Seriously?" I frowned, a little uneasy. Last time we'd snooped around in a suspect's room, we'd almost gotten caught. As it was, we'd wound up jammed nose to nose in a closet. I couldn't imagine getting that lucky a second time. "That's . . . risky."

"It is," Holiday agreed, "but I don't see another way to get the kind of unequivocal proof we're going to need if we want to go to the cops with this."

"Unequivocal proof like what? A signed affidavit? A journal entry that details precisely what he did and how he did it?"

"Greer's watch," she countered, ticking the option. "A piece of paper with his handwriting on it that matches the note. Truly, any number of things." She shook her head. "Anyway, we can't tomorrow, obviously, but if there's a party on Saturday—"

"Why can't we tomorrow?" I asked her—or started to, anyway. I was interrupted by Duncan bounding down the steps of the science building, Harvard beanie slightly askew on his curly head.

"Hey!" he said; then, doing an actual, physical double take: "Holiday!" He shook his head, blushing a little. "Hey, Holiday."

"Hey yourself," Holiday said with a grin. "Duncan."

"What's up?" he asked. His smile was megawatt.

"Not much," she replied. "Just heading to the T."

"Me too!" he said immediately. "Well, not to the T, exactly, but—" He shook his head, looking momentarily confused by his own destination. "Can I walk with you?"

"Sure," she said, already taking a step back toward the sidewalk. "That'd be great." She lifted an eyebrow in my direction, almost imperceptible. "Bye, Michael."

"Bye." I managed not to roll my eyes, but barely. It wasn't like

I didn't understand why he was interested: Holiday was like that, the kind of girl people wanted to be around. Having her full attention felt like standing next to a space heater, warm and occasionally a little bit itchy. "I'll let you know about a party!" I called pointedly, though I wasn't sure either one of them would hear me.

"You do that!" Holiday yelled, without looking back.

11

Saturday, 11/23/24

"IT'S COLD AS BALLS," HOLIDAY ANNOUNCED WHEN I
pushed the heavy door open and found her standing on the brick
pathway outside my building two nights later, the wind blowing
her hair around her face and her olive cheeks rosy in the glow of
the sodium lights. "You ready to go?"

"Hey, Holiday!" Duncan piped up, stopping short right behind me. He'd trailed me downstairs like an Irish wolfhound when
Holiday had texted to say she was here—he was ostensibly on his
way to pick up food at Tasty Burger, though it was clear from the
hopeful, hangdog expression on his face that that was in no way
his actual intention. "You look great."

I rolled my eyes as I jogged down the wide granite steps to
join her, though I couldn't help but notice that it wasn't like Duncan was *wrong*. Holiday's personal style usually skewed toward
"forty-five-year-old mom from Huron Village": big sweaters and
clogs with enormous wooden soles and dresses that could most
accurately be described as frocks, plus the occasional potato-sack

jumpsuit. But she'd dressed the lax-house part tonight, in jeans and boots and a lacy top that was just this side of sheer; she'd done some girl business with her makeup that made her eyes look very dark. "Come on," I said, clearing my throat and jerking my head toward the sidewalk. "We're going this way."

Holiday nodded. "Have a good night, Duncan!" she called, flashing her warmest smile over one perfumed shoulder. "Maybe we'll see you later."

"We will not," I muttered, steering her in the opposite direction. Holiday ignored me.

It took fifteen minutes to walk to the lax house, the bustle of the Square fading behind us as the streets got quieter and more residential, the only sound the bare branches of the oak trees rubbing themselves together overhead. Holiday seemed quiet tonight too, none of her usual running patter about the latest woman playwright in residence at the Huntington or the Intro to Ceramics class she was considering signing up for at the CCAE. It was noticeable enough that finally I glanced over at her in the darkness: "Hey," I said as we crossed an empty side street, "you okay?"

Holiday looked surprised. "Yeah," she said quickly. "Yeah, totally." Then, half a block later: "Can I ask you a question, though? Did something happen last night?"

I glanced at her blankly. "No, why?" Last night had been Friday; I'd gotten dinner with Greer at a ramen place near Central, then gone back to her suite and scrolled football scores on my phone for an hour while she and the other girls did Richard Gere pregame, some sad 2000s rom-com about a middle-aged couple doing ballroom dancing. The rest of them had gone to a party when it was over, but Greer had brought me back to her empty bedroom, locked the door, and let me take her bra off, which—while it *was* the first time that had happened since we'd started hanging out again—was probably not the kind of information Holiday was fishing for. "What would have happened?"

I—" Holiday broke off, then shook her head, turning to sidestep a giant root that had buckled the cobblestone sidewalk. "No, nothing. I just meant, like, Bri-wise."

"Like, with Hunter, you mean?" I racked my brain, scrubbing for anything I might have missed. "No, I don't think so. He'll be here tonight, though, obviously."

Holiday nodded. "Okay," she said. "Well. Good."

Something was up, clearly, and I would have pressed her, but we were already turning onto the long front walk of the lax house. "Duncan was right, PS," I muttered, leaning close to her ear as we climbed the slightly saggy steps to the porch. "You look nice."

Holiday turned to look at me, her red slips slightly parted. Then she shook her head. "Don't sound so surprised," she said with a smirk. "Come on, let's do this thing."

The party was already cranking by the time I opened the front door, the bass from a Lizzo song rattling in my teeth before we even got all the way into the foyer. The lax house was an old Cambridge colonial, with a grand front hall and a formal dining room to one side, Christmas lights crisscrossing the coffered ceilings of the living room.

"There he is!" called Cam, who was sitting on the arm of the sagging leather couch with a Sam Winter in one hand and a joint in the other. "Where you been, Linden?"

Holiday squeezed my arm, already taking a step backward down the hallway that led to the kitchen. "Divide and conquer?" she asked quietly.

"Um, sure," I agreed, a little surprised she was so eager to be left to her own devices in a house full of strangers, though probably I shouldn't have been. No matter how long Holiday and I had known each other, it was always funny to me to watch her at parties—the way she eased equally effortlessly into conversations with sports bros and the daughters of Eastern European oligarchs, making fast friends with party girls and wallflowers alike. There was something utterly unselfconscious about her that people seemed instinctively drawn to—like out of everyone I knew, she was the only one who'd looked at the poster in kindergarten of the tabby cat in sunglasses that said BE YOURSELF and actually taken the advice to heart. Holiday was Holiday, no matter her circumstances. Wherever she went, there she was. It made me a little jealous sometimes, honestly; it felt like there was probably less to remember that way. It freed up the space for her to be so smart about everything else.

I grabbed a beer from an open box on the dining room table and lost her in the crowd for a little while, getting waylaid by a men's rights conspiracy theorist from my International Women Writers class and then distracted by two sophomores improvising a game of pickleball out in the backyard. I was just headed back toward the dining room when Hunter appeared from the direction of the grimy downstairs bathroom and slung a slightly too-rough arm around my shoulders. "Hey, pally," he said. He nodded across the room to where Holiday was perched on the edge of a radiator cover, holding forth with one of our midfielders, a student from Germany who, as far as I could tell, had never said a single word to anyone else. "Who's your friend?"

"That's Holiday," I reported, feeling my entire body coil. "She doesn't go here."

"No kidding," Hunter said with a grin. "I would have noticed."

I scowled. "She has a boyfriend," I lied, then immediately regretted it. It was weird behavior on my part; Holiday would have handed me my ass if she'd overheard, and she would have been right to do so. But seriously, what was the deal with everyone sniffing around her tonight? It was like nobody had ever seen a girl before. "So. You're out of luck, probably."

Hunter shrugged like *What can you do?* before trotting off a moment later, presumably to direct his romantic attention elsewhere or burp into someone's unsuspecting face, one or the other. With Hunter, there was really no way to tell.

I weaved my way through the crowd until I caught Holiday's eye. "Enjoying yourself?" I asked, tugging her into the old telephone nook under the stairs.

"I am, actually." She smiled at me. "The parties have a different vibe at my school."

I glanced down the hallway, wondering what she made of this place. The lax house wasn't grungy, exactly—somebody's dad paid for a cleaning service that came in every week—but it was still unequivocally a place where a bunch of dudes ate and farted and jerked off all day, all of them under one roof. I tried to imagine Holiday's art school parties at people's Beacon Hill apartments decorated like the sets for a Wes Anderson movie, all velvet sofas and clever wallpaper, everyone eating cheese cubes and drinking wine from stemless glasses. All of them talking about Marcel Duchamp. "More Sartre?"

"I mean, no, but it's nice to know that's how you imagine us." She tilted her head toward the kitchen. "Come on," she said. "I scoped out a back staircase off the kitchen."

We made it to the second floor unnoticed; I followed Holiday down the long, dim hallway, the hardwood creaking a little ominously under our feet. The walls were hung with faded photos of the lax teams from back in the '80s and '90s: dozens of mostly indistinguishable white guys with Tom Cruise hair and short shorts and a palpable air of self-satisfaction I tried not to recognize too closely. Was this how people would see me in thirty years? I couldn't help but wonder. Shit, was this how people saw me *now*?

"Which one is Hunter's?" Holiday asked, snapping me back into the present. She motioned to the half-dozen doors that lined the hallway, but I shook my head.

"I have no idea, actually."

"Seriously?" She turned to look at me. "How can you not know?"

"I've never been up here," I admitted. "Only upperclassmen are technically allowed upstairs."

"For the sex parties?"

"Nah, we usually do those in the basement."

"For ease of cleanup," Holiday agreed without missing a trick. "Silly me."

I stood back as she knocked lightly on one door after another, easing them open and nosing around inside until she found ample evidence of their occupants. "What are you going to say if somebody is actually in one of these?" I asked her, glancing nervously over my shoulder in the direction of the stairs.

"That my tampon failed and I'm having a period emergency and I was looking for somewhere private to scrub out my underwear," Holiday said pleasantly. "What are *you* going to say?"

I considered that for a moment. "I mean, same, probably."

Holiday rolled her eyes. "Here we go," she said finally, slipping catlike through a door at the end of the hallway, a corner room with windows on two walls and a gray Ikea rug spread across the scuffed wood floors. Hunter's practice jersey was slung—unwashed, from the smell of it—over the footboard of the bed. "Now we're talking."

I checked the staircase one more time, then stepped in behind her and looked around: a navy-blue quilt and a surprising amount of hair product, a sleek desktop Mac with two monitors sitting on the desk. "Do people still like Vampire Weekend?" I wondered, peering at the posters on the wall with sincere curiosity. "Like, is that a thing?"

"I'm truly the wrong person to ask," Holiday said, making a beeline for the desk. "My most listened-to artist on Spotify last year was Natalie Merchant." She slid the drawers open one by one, poking gingerly through their contents and muttering to herself.

I stood there and watched her for a moment, her lips pursed and her brow furrowed, before catching myself staring and turning abruptly away. I opened the closet door, taking in Hunter's truly impressive collection of Patagonia quarter-zip fleeces, the New Balance sneakers in every color and style. It looked—well, it looked kind of like the inside of my closet, actually, and I glanced over at Holiday, hoping she hadn't noticed.

"Anything useful in there?" she asked, looking at me perfunctorily over one shoulder. "Beyond the fact that you guys evidently have the same personal shopper, I mean."

"Fuck off," I muttered. It wasn't like I cared what Holiday thought of my clothes, exactly. Still, I couldn't help but think of what she'd said that day on the bank of the river, about only hanging out with people who were just like me. "You find anything?"

Holiday shook her head, flicking through a little wire basket next to the computer. "Birthday greeting from Grandma," she reported. "T pass. Gift card to Buffalo Wild Wings." She frowned. "Where is there a Buffalo Wild Wings around here?"

I rolled my eyes. "Holiday—"

"I'm just saying, could be a clue."

"It's not a clue," I said. "Can you just—"

Holiday tutted. "I gotta tell you, Michael," she observed, turning her attention to the nightstand, "I don't feel like you're finding me as charming tonight as you could be."

"I find you, as always, extremely charming," I assured her, glancing nervously in the direction of the closed door. I wasn't sure how long we'd been up here, but it felt like we had to be pushing our luck. "I just don't want to get caught."

"We're not going to—Hang on," Holiday said, still crouched over the nightstand drawer. "Oh, shit."

"What?" I was across the room in two big steps. *"What?"*

"Don't overreact," Holiday said, getting to her feet and

stepping back so I could peer over her shoulder at the contents of the drawer. "And don't touch anything."

"I'm not going to—" I broke off. "Oh, fuck me." In the nightstand drawer, in between a dinged-up tin of lip balm and a tangle of charging cords, was a stack of Polaroids.

Of Greer.

In her underwear.

In bed.

"Woof," Holiday said, nudging around in the rest of the drawer with one manicured finger like she was afraid of catching avian flu. "What a creep." She glanced over at me. "Down, boy."

"I'm not *up,*" I insisted peevishly, then felt myself blush through my deep irritation. I felt a muscle ticing in my jaw. Hunter was a dick, yeah, but he also came from generations of money; his dad was a partner at a hedge fund on Wall Street. His family had a ski house in Vail. I hated to think of him seeing Greer like that at all, let alone whenever he wanted to. I hated the idea of him still having this kind of access. "I mean, I'm not— Whatever. I'm cool."

"Oh yeah, you look real mellow." Holiday nudged me out of the way, pulling her phone out of her pocket. "Her hair is different, right? So they must be from last year?"

"I didn't think they were from this— Whatever," I repeated as she opened up her camera app and snapped a dozen photos of the Polaroids and where we'd found them, stepping back and taking a shot of the nightstand itself for reference. "I mean, this proves it, right? Hunter's still obsessed with Greer. He tried to get back together with her, she turned him down—shit, maybe they even argued about me at some point. He went to her room that night because he knew she wasn't at the party, and thought she might be alo—" I broke off as Holiday slid the nightstand drawer shut. "What are you doing?" My eyes widened. "You're going to *leave* them here?"

Holiday looked at me like I'd lost my mind. "I mean," she said carefully, "I'm not going to steal evidence, no."

"That *evidence* is creepy pictures of my girlfriend that he's probably using to jerk—" I snapped my jaws shut at the unmistakable sound of footsteps coming closer down the hallway.

Holiday's eyes widened. "Fuck," she whispered, her gaze darting wildly around the room. "Is that—?"

"Yeah," I said. "We need to—"

"Hide," she agreed, but the doorknob was already turning.

Just for a second, I froze in a blind, useless panic.

Then I grabbed Holiday around the waist, tossed her down onto Hunter's rumpled bed, and slammed my mouth against hers.

It wasn't elegant. It was spit and teeth and a quiet "oh" from Holiday, our noses bashing together in the second before we course-corrected and her hands came up to cup my face. She opened her mouth, or I did; I could feel how warm her body was, straight through the lacy fabric of her shirt. She was a good kisser, I thought vaguely. I don't know why that surprised me, but it did.

"Hey, are you in h— Whoops!" said a female voice, high and tinkling and openly amused. Holiday and I broke apart—quickly, though probably not as quickly as we could have. I turned around and realized with some horror I was looking back at Noelle, a sophomore who lived a couple of floors above Greer over in Hemlock.

She was wearing a stretchy crop top and big white sneakers and the twisty grin of a person who thinks she's seen something salacious she wasn't supposed to see. "Sorry."

"Shit," I said, pulling back a little dizzily. I didn't need to fake acting stupefied and out of breath. "Uh, no, we're sorry."

"You don't look sorry," Noelle said, still grinning. "As you were." She twirled her hand in a funny little fairy-tale wave before turning and shutting the door neatly behind her.

Once she was gone Holiday cleared her throat, scrambling up off the bed so fast she almost lost her balance and wound up sprawled across it one more time. "Okay," she said, arms pinwheeling a little as she righted herself. "We need to get out of here."

"Uh," I said, getting unsteadily to my feet. I felt like I'd been hit with a two-by-four. I felt like I'd fallen down a well. I'd been working on the beginning of a boner, and I shifted my weight a little awkwardly, hoping Holiday wouldn't notice but knowing that realistically she already had. "Yup."

"Okay," she said again. She was touching her face, her hair, her shirt, her hands migrating up and down her body like a pair of nervous birds searching unsuccessfully for a comfortable place to land. "Well. Let's . . . do that."

She turned on her heel and headed for the door, wrenching it open and marching down the dim, narrow hallway. I stumbled down the staircase after her, tripping a little on the worn carpet runner. Neither of us bothered with our coats. Outside, the porch was littered with empty beer boxes, a couple of empty liquor bottles peeking out of a giant black trash bag. "How are they not worried about this?" Holiday asked, looking around at the detritus.

Her voice was just the tiniest bit shrill. "Like, hasn't it occurred to them that somebody could just be strolling by and see it and call over to the dean like, 'Hey, it's me, Joe Neighbor! Just so you know, there are fifty underage *scholar athletes* getting utterly shit-faced in campus housing and one of them is probably going to get alcohol poisoning or commit a date rape before the evening concludes, okay, have a great night'?"

"This isn't campus housing, technically," I explained, a little taken aback by the hard conversational swerve and also not really loving the air quotes she'd put around "scholar athletes." "And beyond, that, no, I don't think they care that much."

Holiday shook her head. "No," she replied softly. "I guess they wouldn't."

Neither one of us said anything for a moment. A couple of chattering girls got into an Uber a few houses over, their heels clicking on the chilly sidewalk. The wind rustled the branches of the enormous old trees that lined the street. "So what's our next step?" I asked finally, not looking directly at her. Every nerve ending in my body felt open and raw. "We need to bring those photos you took to the cops, right?"

"What?" Holiday asked. Her lips were bright and smudgy in the white glow of the porch light, her hair twice its normal volume, an enormous dark corona around her face. "I—no, I don't think so. Not yet, anyway."

That surprised me. "Wait," I said, "*no*? Why not?"

"I'm not saying never," she amended. "I just want to—"

"Like, what other evidence could we possibly need at this

point?" I asked. Then, when she didn't answer: "Hello? Are you even listening to me right now?"

"Am I—yes!" Holiday snapped. "I'm *flustered,* Michael, will you give me a second?"

I frowned. "Why are you—why, because we—?" I pointed back and forth between us, weirdly unable to say it.

"No!" Holiday exclaimed. Then, seeming to realize that it wasn't an answer that would hold up to even the most casual scrutiny: "I mean, yes, of course because we—" She broke off.

"Okay . . . ," I said uncertainly, feeling an unpleasant heat creeping up out of my collar. "I mean, I'm sorry. I thought it was pretty obvious we needed a cover."

Holiday blew out a breath. "Of course we did, I just—"

"So then why are you mad at me?"

"I'm not *mad* at you," she insisted, in the voice of a person who was definitely, unequivocally mad at me. "I just—"

"You just *what,* exactly?"

"Nothing!" Holiday huffed a noisy breath, raking her tangle of hair back. "Whatever. It's fine. Like you said, we needed a cover."

"I know," I agreed, aware that my own voice was kind of obnoxious but not particularly caring. I felt guilty and defensive without quite knowing why—it was like she was accusing me of something, but only vaguely, leaving me half a set of clues. "I mean, I just hope it doesn't get back to Greer."

Holiday made a face at that, leaning back against the porch railing. "Well," she promised, "she won't hear it from me, I can promise you that much." She jammed her hands into the pockets of her giant sweater—or she tried to, anyway, except she wasn't wearing a giant sweater with pockets, she was wearing a shirt with fiddly little fabric-covered buttons and a neckline I'd been trying not to look at all night long. "Okay," she said, wiping her palms on the seat of her jeans instead. "Anyway."

"Anyway," I agreed, only to snap my jaws shut one more time as the front door of the lax house creaked open, a couple of guys from the team looking at us a little oddly as they ambled out. Probably this wasn't the ideal venue for a private conversation about whether or not our star forward was also possibly a cold-blooded killer. "Anyway," I repeated once they were gone, more quietly this time. "Tell me again why you don't think we should go to the police?"

"Honestly?" Holiday shrugged. "I'm not convinced Hunter's our guy."

"*What?*" I whirled on her, a wave of disbelief and annoyance crashing over me like the ocean slamming into the rocks at Spectacle Island in winter. "You're shitting me."

"I'm not," she said. "And we've made the mistake of going off half-cocked in the past, so this time I want to be sure—"

"You mean *I've* gone off half-cocked." I cringed at the memory of how I'd acted back on Martha's Vineyard, immediately irritated at her for even bringing it up. "This isn't like that."

"Are you sure?" Holiday pressed, then continued before I could answer. "Can I ask you something? Do you like Hunter as a suspect so much because you actually think he killed Bri, or do you like him as a suspect so much because you let him bully you into drinking a goldfish and he slept with Greer while you guys were broken up?"

Oh, that pissed me off. "First of all, he didn't bully me into anything," I informed her, heading toward her across the sagging porch. "I drank that goldfish because I wanted to. And second of all, I like him as a suspect so much because he was verifiably at the crime scene the night of the murder and he's got pictures of my girlfriend in her underwear in his desk like a fucking freak!"

"If it *was* even a crime scene," Holiday shot back.

That stopped me. "What?"

"I'm just saying." Holiday folded her arms and stepped neatly past me, pacing back and forth across the porch. She was shivering; it was freezing out here, though I'd been too distracted to register the cold until right now. "We need to *think* for a minute, okay? We need to be rational and strategic about this. We can't just go careening all over the place, following your every random impulse wherever it takes us." She was talking fast, cheeks flushed and eyes bright when she turned to face me. "I don't even know what's real and what's not, here."

All at once I felt myself get very, very still. "Holiday," I said. "What are we actually talking about right now?"

"What?" Holiday blanched, a look of sheer unadulterated panic crossing her face in the half second before she blinked it away. "Nothing. I mean, we're talking about the case, obviously." She shook her head like she was trying to clear it, pressing the heels of her hands into her eyes. "I'm not thinking clearly," she admitted. "Maybe I drank too much."

I frowned. "Did you drink anything? I didn't drink anything."

"That's not the point, Michael!" Holiday threw her hands up. "Look," she said finally, "we got what we came for, right? We've got the photos. And there's no harm in taking a day or two to figure out whether or not that's enough to get us . . . wherever it is we're trying to go." She sighed. "In the meantime, I'm going to take off. I'll see you at the game tomorrow, okay?"

"Right," I said. The annual Harvard-Yale game was the following morning, this year's matchup in a football rivalry dating back to 1875. It was an all-day affair, the tailgating starting pretty much as soon as the sun came up, the Square filled with wealthy alumni from both universities eager to relive their glory days. On the way over here we'd passed a middle-aged guy in loafers and pleated khakis getting kicked out of a bar on Mass Ave while singing the Yale fight song at the top of his lungs. "Look, Holiday—"

"Yeah?" This was quick.

"I—" I broke off. I wanted to apologize to her, but I couldn't decide what for, exactly. Kissing her, I guess, but I wasn't actually sorry for that. I'd meant what I said—we'd needed a cover— but there was also a part of me that had always wondered what it might be like, that had looked over at her a million times in the car and in the library and on the Charles River Esplanade and thought: *What if?* Now I knew—I didn't think I'd ever be able to unknow it, honestly—but still in some strange way it felt like the wondering itself was the thing I ought to be sorry for. "Are we okay?" I finally asked.

Holiday's shoulders dropped. "We're fine, Michael." She

sounded so much more unsure than I ever thought of her as being. "I'm cold. I'm tired. I just want to go, okay?"

"Let me at least get you a ride back to your dorm."

Holiday shook her head. "We're like three blocks from my house," she reminded me. "I'm just going to crash there tonight."

"I—oh." She was right, I realized suddenly. I had never thought of it like that; the illusion of an independent adult life on campus was so all-consuming that most of the time it felt like I was a whole world away from the places where I'd grown up, but of course she was right—we were, at most, a seven-minute walk from her parents' massive Cambridge Victorian. Holiday could probably do it in five. I could picture the house so clearly: the dark paint crisp and fresh against the row of perfectly trimmed evergreen bushes lining the wraparound porch, the trio of Adirondack chairs festooned with seasonally appropriate outdoor pillows. The front door was always flanked by clusters of fat orange and white pumpkins at this time of year, dozens of them spilling down the wide front steps: my mom had probably arranged them, same as she did every autumn, picking them up at Pemberton Farms and lugging them out of her trunk one by one.

It didn't *feel* like we were three blocks from Holiday's parents' house, though. All of a sudden it felt like we were very far from home.

"Well," I said at last, rocking back on my heels a little. "Okay. Text me when you get there, anyway."

Holiday smiled at that, just faintly. "I will text you when I get there," she promised.

I walked her as far as the sidewalk in silence, watching as her tall, broad figure receded into the darkness and reminding myself there was no reason to feel like I was never going to see her again.

Then: "Oh, shit," I realized suddenly. "Holiday!" I called. "Wait!"

Even as she turned to look at me I dashed back into the house and darted through the crowd in the kitchen, finally finding her coat near the bottom of the pile in the old butler's pantry. I grabbed mine too; I'd go with her, I decided with wild conviction, imagining the two of us sitting side by side on the couch in her parents' book-lined den and watching some stupid movie on their extravagant cable package until things between us felt safe and normal again.

I careened back out into the chilly night, catching up with her half a block away, where she was standing underneath a streetlamp, the cold light bouncing off her glossy hair. "Here," I said breathlessly, holding the coat out in her direction.

Her eyes widened in recognition. "Thank you," she said, shrugging it on and immediately tucking her hands into the pockets.

"You're welcome," I said. Then, summoning courage from somewhere deep behind my ribcage: "Look," I said, "what if I just—"

"Yo, Linden!"

I turned around: back at the lax house, Cam was leaning against the porch rail, his posture loose and drunk, his face friendly. "You coming back inside?" he asked, the clang and clatter of the party rending the quiet night. "We're gonna play beer pong."

I considered that for a moment, looking from him to Holiday and back again, down at my own jacket still clutched in my hand.

I could feel the courage leaching out of me like runoff from one of those old Fall River glove factories. "Um," I said finally, my voice as casual as I could manage. "Yeah. I'll be there in a sec."

Cam nodded. "Suit yourself," he said, the door slamming behind him as he went back inside.

Holiday was already stepping away by the time I turned around again, ducking out of the glow from the streetlight and into the darkness so I couldn't see her face. "Night, Michael," she said softly.

"Night, Holiday."

I stood there on the sidewalk for a long time once she was gone, knowing I'd missed something important. Knowing I'd let a chance slip away. I didn't actually want to go back inside and play beer pong, and finally I got tired of lurking around under a streetlight like a total boner, so in the end I shrugged my jacket on and headed back in the direction of my dorm. I took the long way, passing graveyards from the 1700s and big old houses with warm yellow light glowing through their front windows, breathing in the smell of a fire in someone's far-off fireplace and telling myself I felt nothing at all.

12

Sunday, 11/24/24

HOLIDAY LET HERSELF INTO MY DORM ROOM THAT
night while I was sleeping, easing the door open and padding
across the industrial carpet in a soft pair of sweats. "Hi," she muttered, reaching out and running the tip of her index finger along
the curve of my ear, a touch so light it seemed wildly improbable
that I could feel it all over my body.

"Hi," I said, boosting myself up onto my elbows as she climbed
into bed with me, slinging one leg over my hips and making herself comfortable. She smelled different than usual, flowery and
faint. "What are you doing?"

Holiday grinned, her smile like a slice of moonlight in the
dark. "What do you think?" She reached back and pulled her shirt
off—

And I woke up with a gasp alone in my extra-long twin bed.

"Dude," Dave said, glancing at me across the room from his
perch in his desk chair, where he was scrolling a thread on Dis-
cord and eating a banana. Dave was from South Korea by way of

California; his parents sent elaborate care packages full of socks and ginger tea. "You good?"

"I'm awesome," I muttered, then counted to a hundred and shuffled grumpily down the hall toward the bathroom. "Never better."

The weather that day was perfect for a football game: crisp and clear and sunny, the kind of autumn morning that made me feel nostalgic about living in New England, even though I was still actively doing it. The streets were packed with tourists. The air smelled like leaves. A guy dressed in full Revolutionary War regalia handed out pamphlets advertising walking tours of Harvard Square.

Holiday had texted to say she'd meet me at the entrance to the stadium, and when I made my way over she was already waiting, looking more like her regular self today in a big cream-colored fisherman's sweater. I felt myself relax at the sight of her in broad daylight, tall and lipsticked and *normal:* it had been an aberration, that was all, whatever had happened between us last night. It didn't have to change anything.

"Look," I said as soon as we were close enough. "About—"

"I was tired," Holiday interrupted with a wave of her hand, "and I listened to *Dear Evan Hansen* right before I came to the party. You were totally fine."

"Are you sure?" I asked uncertainly. "Because it definitely felt like—"

"*Michael,*" she said; I couldn't tell if I was imagining the edge in her voice or not. "You're good. Seriously. I would have done the same thing if you hadn't gotten there first."

"You would?" I asked, half a beat too quickly. "I mean, you would have—" I broke off.

Holiday looked suspicious all of a sudden, like possibly she thought I was setting some kind of trap for her. "Anyway," she said instead of answering, "there's something else I want to talk to you about. I was thinking when I got home last night: Why was that girl Noelle—"

"Linden!" Greer called. When I looked up she was ambling toward us along with the rest of her suitemates, all of them looking like something out of a promotional brochure from the Office of Undergraduate Admissions in their jeans and Harvard sweatshirts. "Hi!"

I introduced Holiday around as we met up with a couple of the guys from the lax team and a few other people from Hemlock, all of us climbing the tall stadium steps to our seats. "I've heard a lot about you," Holiday told Greer, and though her tone was perfectly friendly, her smile wide, something about the way she said it had my gaze flicking nervously in her direction.

"You have?" Greer asked, glancing back at me sidelong. "How do you guys know each other?"

"We grew up together" was all Holiday said, then shaded her eyes with one hand as she peered down at the concession stand. "Anybody want lemonade?"

It was fun, the Harvard-Yale game, everybody in a celebratory, almost-Thanksgiving kind of mood; we cheered and swore and drank the party punch Margot had snuck into the stadium in a water bladder, Greer's arm looped casually around my waist. We headed down the bleachers for popcorn at halftime, her phone

pinging with a text as we waited in line: "Be right back," she promised, though she hadn't returned by the time I finished paying, and
eventually I found her near the entrance gates, talking urgently to
a girl in ripped black jeans and a flannel.

"Hey!" she said as I approached, taking the popcorn with a
grateful smile. "You remember my cousin Emily, right?"

I didn't, actually—I didn't think we'd ever met, back at
Bartley—though she did look weirdly familiar to me, with blond
hair and a spray of freckles across her fair, angular face. "How's it
going?" I asked, holding my hand out. "You don't go here, do you?
Are you at Yale?"

"She's at BU," Greer reported.

"I am," Emily agreed, eyes still on Greer, "although honestly
we hardly ever see each other, since my cousin here can only be
bothered to return like one out of every three texts."

"Not true!" Greer protested, her mouth dropping open. "We
see each other."

Emily raised an eyebrow. "Do we, though?" she asked sweetly.

"We definitely do," Greer said. Then, not quite under her
breath: "We see each other plenty."

I wasn't sure what *that* meant, exactly, though if Emily was
anything like the rest of Greer's family I could probably guess.
"What are you studying?" I asked Emily, trying to change the subject. "At BU, I mean."

Emily lifted her chin like a challenge. "As it happens, I'm
undeclared."

"Me too," I admitted. "Although I like to think of it more as
keeping my options open."

We chatted a little while longer, about the game and about their family Thanksgiving, which their grandma was hosting back in Connecticut; I was just about to ask if they were driving down together when Holiday came up behind me and put a hand on my shoulder. "Hey," she said over the roar of the crowd. "Can I borrow you for a sec?"

"Oh!" I said, surprised. Honestly, I'd almost forgotten Holiday was here: I wasn't sure whether or not it had anything to do with what had happened the night before, but she'd kept her distance for most of the first half of the game, chatting with Dagny and Celine and Margot; I'd briefly clocked her talking to Li-Wen, a sophomore who lived in the same suite in Hemlock as Noelle and a couple of other girls from the crew team, then lost track of her again. "Sure."

I promised Greer and Emily I'd catch up with them soon and followed Holiday through the crowd and down underneath the bleachers, blinking as my eyes adjusted to the dimness. The game was muffled down here, the air a full ten degrees colder. "Who was that girl you were talking to?" she asked. "The blond?"

For one utterly unhinged second I thought she was asking because she was jealous. "Greer's cousin Emily," I reported. "Why?"

"She looks familiar to me from someplace," Holiday mused, tugging thoughtfully on the end of one dark curl, "but I don't know where I would have seen her."

"To me too, actually," I admitted. "But yeah, I don't know from where. She goes to BU, if that helps. Is that what you wanted to talk to me about?"

"No, actually." Holiday shook her head. "Hunter's not our guy."

"What the fuck?" I blinked, snagged by the suddenness of it. "Wait, how do you know that? How can you possibly know that?"

Holiday sighed. "So that's what I was trying to tell you before the game started," she said. "All last night, I was wondering what that girl Noelle was doing barging into Hunter's room without knocking. You know, when she walked in on—" She waved a hand back and forth between us, blushing a little.

"I think I recall, yes."

"It made me wonder if there was something going on between them, which"—she pulled out her phone and clicked over to Noelle's Instagram, shoving a picture of Hunter in my face—"ta-da, there does actually seem to be. And I knew from that big list you made for me a few weeks ago that Noelle lives in Hemlock, so. It's a pretty safe bet that's what—or, you know, *who*—Hunter was doing in Hemlock House the night that Bri died."

Right away, I shook my head. "It's conjecture," I argued, echoing her words from the night before. "We still don't know for sure."

"We do," Holiday countered. "Li-Wen explicitly told me. She said that the night Bri died she had to crash in the common room of their suite because whatever Noelle and Hunter were getting up to sounded like, and I quote, 'someone was eating a bowl of pudding without the benefit of a spoon.'"

I winced. "Oh, my god."

"She should be a creative writing major, right?" Holiday said admiringly. "I told her she belongs at my school instead."

"She certainly has a way with words," I had to admit.

"Anyway," Holiday continued, "Hunter didn't do it.'

"Okay," I said, trying without a ton of success to swallow a surge of annoyance. "Well, that's that, then. We are, and continue to be, absolutely nowhere."

"I mean, don't get pissed."

"I'm not," I said irritably. I was, though. I was pissed at Hunter for those pictures. I was pissed at Holiday for always being one step ahead. I was pissed at myself about that dream, and for kissing her to begin with, for cracking a door we both knew was better off staying firmly shut.

"I know you wanted it to be him," she continued, tucking her hands into her back pockets. "But it wasn't."

"I didn't *want* it to be him," I said, a little defensive. It was the same voice she'd used to tell me that one weird note did not a murder mystery make. She'd been wrong about that, though, hadn't she? She'd been wrong, and I'd been right. "I'm just frustrated that now—"

"Everything okay?" Greer asked just then, her Bean boots crunching on the gravel as she came up behind us. It was hard to see her expression in the dimness, but her tone was definitely the tone of a person who'd come to make sure nothing untoward was going on between her ex-boyfriend/current hookup and his tall, striking childhood friend.

"Everything's great," Holiday said brightly, evidently choosing not to acknowledge the inherent weirdness of the two of us huddling together under a set of literal bleachers like something out of a musical sequence from *Grease*. "I was just about to go."

Greer frowned. "In the middle of the game?"

"Oh, I'm not a football person. I think undergraduate sports should be illegal, actually." Holiday smiled winningly. "It was nice to finally meet you, Greer! See you around, I hope." She turned to me, then hesitated for a fraction of a moment before nodding, the gesture oddly businesslike and formal. "Michael. I'll talk to you."

We watched as she marched away, both of us a little bit gobsmacked by the Holiday of it all. "What was happening there?" Greer asked once she was gone.

Our murder investigation just went entirely to shit, on top of which I think she's mad at me for kissing her in Hunter's room at the lax party last night was not an answer I felt comfortable giving, so instead, I just shrugged like *Theater girls, am I right?* "Nothing," I promised, rolling my eyes a little. "She's just . . . It's a long story."

"A long story like we're a long story?"

I tipped my head to the side, cautious. "Are we a long story?"

"I didn't think so." She raised an eyebrow. "Are you guys a thing?" she asked. "You and Holiday? Or like, *were* you a thing while we were broken up, if you're not a thing now?"

I almost laughed, but then it abruptly stopped being funny and the sound I made was like a weird, guilty, strangled burp. "What?" I asked shrilly. "No."

I had never in my life seen Greer look less impressed. "So, yes?"

"No!" I insisted. "*No,* not at all. We're friends. We've been friends since we were little." I took a breath. "My mom is her housekeeper, actually. Her family's housekeeper."

That stopped her, which had admittedly been the point. At the back of my mind I felt a little dirty for using the awkward novelty of my mom's blue-collar job to distract Greer from an argument—though not, apparently, dirty enough not to do it. "I— Oh," she said, nodding so fast and hard she looked like a Harvard-themed bobblehead. "That's cool."

"Yeah." I cleared my throat. "Anyway, there's nothing going on between Holiday and me. We were just—I mean, she's been helping me try to figure out—" I broke off.

Greer's eyes narrowed one more time. "What?" she prompted.

"No, nothing."

"Linden." She huffed out a little laugh, high and nervous. "What the fuck?"

"I'm sorry," I said, "I'm sorry." I shook my head, and then I said it. "Look," I said, "can I ask you—do you think there's any chance that what happened to Bri wasn't an accident?"

All at once Greer got very, very still. "What do you mean?" she asked. "Like she overdosed on *purpose*? No, Linden. She wouldn't have—I mean, she wasn't, like depressed, or—"

"No no no," I clarified. "That's not what I meant."

"Then what did you mean?"

"Like, was there something wrong with her drugs, maybe," I posited, though at this point I was pretty sure the pills had just been a decoy. "Or was she, you know. Like. Suffocated."

"*What?*" Greer gaped at me. "Are you deranged?"

"I don't know," I told her honestly. "I just—"

"Wouldn't the police have been able to tell?"

"I don't think the police are looking," I said. "Do you think the police are looking?"

"I mean, no?" Greer said. "I don't think so? I don't think there was any reason to—I have no idea! And I also have no idea why you're being such a weirdo right now. Like, what are you even—"

"The whole thing just seems strange, is all."

"It *is* strange!" Greer exploded. "My whole life is strange right now! Bri was my best friend, Linden, and she's *dead*. I don't get to talk to her before we fall asleep at night or get ready together to go out or have her bring me a snack from the dining hall if I don't feel like going myself. She's just *gone*. She's not, like, a brain teaser for you and your weird friend to work out."

"No, of course not," I said. "I just—"

Greer put her hands to her cheeks, like that painting of the guy screaming; her braid was unraveling a little, her dark hair starting to frizz around her face. "Look," she interrupted. "I heard about that thing on the Vineyard a couple summers ago, with Jasper's family. I know you had like, a friend involved. Was that Holiday too?"

I hesitated, but there was no point in trying to lie. "I mean, yeah, but—"

"Okay." Greer cut me off, her whole body straightening with barely contained anger. "I don't know if you guys think you're a couple of crack amateur PIs now or what, but this is real life, do you understand that? You weren't there when Bri's parents showed up. You didn't have to watch while they carried her stuff out crying. You haven't had to walk around campus for the last few weeks knowing that the first thing anyone thinks when they see you is *Oh, there's that girl whose roommate OD'd in her* fucking bed."

"No no no," I said quickly. "I know, and I don't mean to—I'm not trying to—" I broke off. "Greer, I'm just trying to protect you."

"Protect *me*?" Greer's eyes narrowed. "From what?"

"Holiday and I—" I sighed, scrubbing a hand through my hair and knowing that there was absolutely no way this was about to improve the conversation. The second half of the game had started, I could hear it: the shriek of a whistle, the hollering of the crowd. "We think it's possible that Bri wasn't the real, um. Target."

"*Target?*" Greer laughed, but a little hysterically, the sound of it brittle as shale. "Oh, my god. Oh, my *god.* Is that why you were asking my suitemates all those weird questions about Hunter wanting to hurt me?"

"It wasn't—I mean—" I winced, although what had I expected, really? Of course they'd reported that back to her. "Hunter is probably in the clear, actually, for what it's worth. He was with Noelle from the sixth floor at the time Bri was—" I stopped short, not wanting to say it. "He was with Noelle from the sixth floor."

Greer shook her head, looking at me like she'd never seen me before. Looking like she had no idea what to do with me at all. "I've gotta go," she announced suddenly. "I've got like a hundred pages of reading for tomorrow that I haven't even started. I don't even know why I came to this stupid game. College sports *should* be illegal, actually. Your creepy friend Holiday is right."

"Greer—"

But Greer wasn't listening. "Maybe we've been moving too fast," she said, backing away slowly, like I was the dangerous one; a sliver of sunlight slipped through the bleachers, just catching the side of her face. "Everything has been so out of control, and *I've* felt so out of control. . . ." She trailed off. "Let's just talk after the break, okay?"

That stopped me. "But wait," I said, "what about Maine?" We were still supposed to spend Thanksgiving weekend up at Margot's family camp near Camden; the plan was for Greer to go home to Connecticut for the actual holiday, then pick me up in Boston on Friday afternoon. When I'd told my mom about it she hadn't fought me, but the expression on her face was the one she got when she was actively trying not to react to something, and later that night when I was looking at Instagram, I saw that she'd reposted a poem about birds flying south for the winter that made me feel kind of like a dick.

Now, though, Greer hesitated. "I don't know, Linden," she said, not quite looking at me. "I think maybe it's better if we just take the long weekend to cool off."

I felt my heart drop into my stomach. "I'm cool," I promised quickly. "Greer. Hey. I'm cool."

But Greer shook her head. "I'll text you when I'm back, okay? Have a good Thanksgiving."

She'd turned and disappeared into the crowd before I could reply.

I stayed there for a long moment, head dropped back and hands shoved into my pockets. How the hell had I managed to bungle that so badly? I was just about to run after her, to tell her I had no idea what I was talking about, to beg her to forgive me, when all at once I froze where I was standing, realizing in a cold flash of clarity where I'd seen Greer's cousin Emily before: she was the girl who'd held the front door for me as she was stomping out of Hemlock House the day Greer and I had gone to Castle Island.

Right after Greer's room had been trashed.

13

Monday 11/25/24–Friday 11/29/24

I BARELY SLEPT THAT NIGHT, OR THE ONE THAT CAME after it. I kept replaying my conversation with Greer in my head, wondering how I could have handled it differently. I kept replaying the other night in Hunter's room.

I dozed off in International Women Writers on Tuesday morning, I couldn't help it; I woke up just as the lecture was wrapping, startling to alertness as my classmates packed their things all around me. I swallowed down the stale, sticky taste in my mouth, slinging my backpack over my shoulder and trying to sneak out of the hall as unobtrusively as possible.

No such luck: "Michael," Professor McMorrow called just as I was heading through the door, "hang on a minute, will you?"

I bit my tongue, barely suppressing a visible wince. This was the last conversation I was ready to have, especially now; all I wanted to do was shuffle back to Eastie, stuff myself full of turkey and sleep for four full days. "I know," I said once the classroom was empty, more sharply than I meant to. "I owe you a meeting."

McMorrow nodded. "You do, although actually I just wanted to pull you aside to ask you, going forward, to find another venue to catch up on your Zs."

"Uh, yeah." I winced. "Sorry about that."

"I understand you've had a lot going on," she continued. "I'm not sure if you got my email about your friend Bri, but—"

"I did," I said, remembering with a sudden surge of irritation the way everyone on campus had tried to pump me for information after she died. "It just wasn't really something I wanted to talk about."

McMorrow nodded. "Fair enough," she said. "But all first-years do need to meet with their advisor before the end of the semester, and in terms of registering for your classes for the spring, it would be good for us to sit down and—"

"Let's just have it now," I interrupted. "The meeting, I mean. I have no idea what classes I want to take next semester. I have no idea what I want my major to be. I have no idea about a lot of things, honestly, including what I'm doing here most days, so I don't know that it makes a ton of sense for us to schedule something just to sit and waste each other's time."

"Well." McMorrow's eyebrows twitched. "I'm sorry to hear that you're struggling. That's all the more reason for—"

"I'm not *struggling*," I said, weirdly offended by the suggestion. "I just—" I broke off. I just *what*, exactly? I just completely alienated my girlfriend by spending the last three weeks on a murder investigation that probably isn't even legitimate? I just kissed my best friend in a panicky attempt at an undercover operation and now she won't look me in the eye? All at once it occurred to me that I was flailing. All at once it occurred to me that I was way out of line. "I'm sorry," I said, holding my hands up. "That wasn't— I shouldn't have—"

"Michael," McMorrow said, and her voice was surprisingly gentle. "Are you sure you don't want to talk?"

"I'll email you," I promised—hands still up, taking two giant steps back toward the doorway. "We'll set something up."

I bailed out of the lecture hall before she could reply.

❧

The dorms closed for Thanksgiving break at noon on Wednesday, my classmates grumbling good-naturedly about traffic or the crowds at airport on the busiest travel days of the year. For my part I packed up a duffel and took the T back home to Eastie, trying not to feel sorry for myself. Normally, Thanksgiving was my favorite holiday; in fact, it had always been kind of a special thing for my mom and me, the two of us making a gross-but-delicious green bean casserole and watching the dog show on TV, then driving down to Revere Beach to watch the sunset and eat pie in the car while listening to Christmas carols on Lite FM. We did all those things this year too, but none of it felt especially festive. I couldn't stop thinking about Greer, the accusing look in her eyes under the bleachers at the football game.

Also, I couldn't stop thinking about Holiday.

I'd texted to tell her what I suspected about Emily, and she'd agreed it was worth looking into, though it wasn't totally clear how to do that when Greer wasn't speaking to me and we didn't know Emily's last name. We found one promising profile among Greer's Instagram followers, EmilyBoo42, but the account was set to private and the avatar pic was a screenshot of Miss Piggy in an evening gown.

Neither one of us had mentioned the kiss again.

"So, obviously I recognize that you'd rather fling yourself directly into the Mystic River than talk to me about girl stuff," my mom said finally, tucking one leg underneath her in the driver's seat and taking a bite of her pie, "but you know I'm here to listen if you want." She held her hand out. "Switch."

"You're right," I said, passing her my big plastic clamshell. My mom was a good baker, but she hated to do it, so we always got two different pies from Market Basket and ate them whole without bothering to slice them; I'd picked pumpkin every single year since I was seven, but for her part she liked to mix it up. This year she'd gotten banana cream. "I'd rather die." I licked the back of my fork—the bananas were a little gloopy, but not necessarily in a bad way. "Also, what makes you think I'm having girl trouble?"

My mother eyed me across the gear shift. "Aren't you?"

I spent that night and the better part of the following morning on the ancient Bernie & Phyl's sofa in our living room, watching a Lord of the Rings marathon on cable even though I've never entirely been able to follow the plot of Lord of the Rings. "That's because Lord of the Rings is excruciatingly boring," my mom explained when I mentioned it to her, padding through the living room with a basket of laundry on one hip. "Inevitably, you fall asleep and miss something, but you don't realize that's what happened because every scene looks exactly the same."

I was opening my mouth to agree when the doorbell rang downstairs. "It's me," Holiday said, when I hit the button on the staticky old intercom. When I opened the door a moment later she was standing on the other side of it in leggings and a pair of filthy Ugg boots she'd had since eighth grade. "Hi," she said.

"Hi," I said cautiously. Her expression was perfectly normal, but I didn't know if that was because she was *feeling* perfectly normal or because she was still mad at me for kissing her and trying to act like she wasn't. "How was Thanksgiving?"

"My mom doesn't believe in Thanksgiving," Holiday reminded me, skirting past me into the living room. "We do a land acknowledgment and then she goes to the outlet mall in Wrentham." She shrugged, holding up a paper bag from Spinelli's. "I brought lunch."

"You always have been a girl after my own heart," my mom said, coming into our tiny foyer and dropping a kiss on Holiday's cheek. "Hi, honey. Michael, take her coat, will you?"

"I can get my own coat," Holiday told me.

"I know," I said, and took it anyway.

"So what's up?" I asked, once we'd eaten our sandwiches and Holiday had gamely answered my mom's ten thousand questions about college. I led her down the narrow hallway to my room and shut the door behind me, then thought twice and opened it again. "Did you come up with something?"

Holiday looked at me a little weirdly. "What do you mean?"

"Did you—" I broke off. "I mean, about Emily."

"No," she said. Her eyes narrowed. "Why?"

"No, no reason," I said too quickly. "I mean, I just figured you came over to tell me something. About . . . Emily."

"No," Holiday said again, crossing her arms warily. She was wearing a purple hoodie with *Emerson College Football: Undefeated Since 1880* printed across the front. "I just came over to . . . come over."

"Okay," I said, wincing at the awkwardness of it. Fuck, why was this so hard all of a sudden? All summer it had been totally normal, but now—"Well, good. I'm glad you did."

"Okay."

We were silent for a moment. Holiday glanced around my room. That summer we'd spent most of our time out in the city or over at her house, and I didn't think she'd been in here in six or seven years at least. "Animorphs," she observed, gazing at the pictures taped to the wall behind my computer. "Very nice."

"Fuck off," I said with a grin. Once I'd moved into the dorms at Bartley I'd more or less curated my entire identity like some kind of monthly subscription box, surrounding myself with items that matched the tastes of the person I was trying to be: arty, minimalist movie posters I'd ordered off the internet and fancy soap from the obnoxious general store in Great Barrington. Here I hadn't bothered with any of that, so the whole aesthetic was frozen in middle-school purgatory. "Anyway, that's nothing. Wait until we revisit my extensive collection of manga."

In the end we wound up sitting on the floor and playing Catan for a full hour while 96.9 played Boston's Best Throwbacks on the Mickey Mouse clock radio I'd had since I learned to tell time.

It was weirdly fun, both of us expanding our road networks and shit-talking each other's resource production. It reminded me of when we were little kids and my mom would set us up with some kind of project, mixing up a batch of morning glory muffins from a crunchy kids' cookbook she'd gotten in the used books basement at Harvard Book Store or bringing her all the things we could find in Holiday's backyard that started with the letter *L*. It reminded me of how I'd felt at the end of the day back at Bartley, when I could finally take off my coat and tie.

The afternoon passed, gray winter light filtering in through the window. My mom made us a bowl of popcorn sprinkled with nutritional yeast. My aunt Rose called from Cincinnati to wish us a happy Thanksgiving, which she'd forgotten to do the day before because she'd been the on-call nurse in the emergency room, and my mom's laughter echoed down the hall as they talked.

"Did you hear from your dad?" Holiday asked quietly, rolling the dice on the matted carpet. "Yesterday, I mean?"

I snorted. "No." My dad hadn't called in ages. Last I knew, he was living outside Denver with a girlfriend who usually tucked some cash into my birthday cards before signing them on his behalf, but it was possible they'd broken up because I hadn't gotten one of those in a couple of years. It didn't really bother me that much, except when it did.

"Well, that sucks," Holiday said, setting a development card down on the carpet. "I'm sorry. And I'm sorry about Greer too."

"No you're not."

"Excuse you." Right away, her head snapped up. "What's *that* supposed to mean?"

"Relax," I said quickly, holding both hands out. "I just mean—I know you didn't think she was, like. Expanding my personal horizons, or whatever."

"*You* don't expand *my* personal horizons, and I like you fine."

"Fuck you!" I said with a laugh. "I'm at fuckin' Harvard. I'm a genius, as far as you're concerned."

"Fuck you," she echoed fondly. "I'm kidding. I think you are a genius, actually. Or you could be, if you wanted it bad enough."

"And you don't think I want it bad enough?"

Holiday looked at me for a long moment. "No," she said finally, and her voice was so quiet. "I don't think you do." She cleared her throat. "Why did you guys break up? The first time, I mean."

I glanced at her a little sharply; we'd never talked about it, and I hesitated, wondering exactly how much I wanted to tell her. "Things got kind of weird after the accident. She was, uh. The one driving the car, so."

"*Oh.*" Holiday's eyes widened, though I could tell she was trying not to react. "I . . . didn't know that."

"I don't talk about it that much." I hardly ever talked about it at all, actually, to Holiday or to anyone else—one, because every time I thought about it I wound up pissed-off and cranky, and two, because Greer and I had lied to everyone at Bartley about what we were doing when it happened, and in my experience the best way to keep a lie straight was not to talk about it in the first place. Still, Holiday sat silently, ankles crossed on the carpet; both of us knew she was waiting me out, and both of us knew it would eventually work.

"The rules about cars at Bartley are weird," I explained finally.

"Seniors are allowed to have them, but it's this complicated thing where you're not really like, supposed to take them very far unless you're driving home for a break? Like, they're called town privileges, but that's it." I shrugged. "Anyway, the night of the accident we told everyone we went to see a movie at the second-run theater."

"But you didn't."

I shook my head. "I thought we were going to, but then at the last minute she said she had a personal thing to handle, and she wanted me to come with her. We drove back toward Boston and she met up with . . . somebody."

"To do what?"

"I don't know, exactly." My recollection of the whole night was hazy; it had taken the better part of a year for my short-term memory to sort itself out. "We were out somewhere near Alewife, I think, in one of those big shopping centers that has like a Target and a Trader Joe's. It was raining. She had me wait in the car, but I could kind of see her from the passenger seat."

"But you don't know who or why?"

I frowned. "Whoever it was, they were wearing a parka, and I only saw them for a second. And like I said, the weather was shit. Anyway, by the time we got back out toward campus it was late, almost curfew, and I think we both were kind of worried about getting caught. I tried to get her to tell me who she'd met up with, and she wouldn't. We argued—we *were* arguing—when we hit the deer." I shrugged. "You can kind of fill in the blanks. My ankle was busted, I couldn't play the rest of spring semester, she felt guilty, I was trying not to act like I was mad at her, but I probably *was* a little mad at her. . . ." I trailed off. "We just kind of drifted."

Holiday nodded slowly. "And you never asked what the deal was?"

I shook my head. I knew she was wondering why I hadn't pushed—why I hadn't investigated—but before I could explain how fragile things had felt with Greer back then, not to mention how tenuous they still sometimes felt with her *now,* my mom was knocking on the open door, waving her phone at me and telling me I needed to talk to Rose; then I was *on* the phone with Rose for ten full minutes, and by the time I hung up, my mom and Holiday had decided we should look at photo albums from when Holiday and I were kids, the two of them hauling them out of the cabinet in the entertainment unit and cracking them open. "We look like the Little Rascals," Holiday said, and we actually sort of did, her with her wild hair and poking-out stomach, me with what was clearly the remainder of a Popsicle dripping down the bottom half of my face.

"What was the name of the place near your house where we used to get the Italian ices?" I asked. My mom had gone back into the kitchen with her laptop to work on a diaper drive for her mutual aid group; it was just Holiday and me, the album open between us on the floor. "With the weird sad rabbit in the cage in the window?"

Holiday wrinkled her nose. "In retrospect, that situation was . . . not hygienic," she said with a grimace. "Also, we probably should have called the MSPCA."

"You *did* call the MSPCA," I reminded her with a laugh. "Remember? You left them an anonymous tip."

"Oh, my god, I did." Holiday clapped a hand over her mouth. "I wonder if that's why it closed."

"Gone forever, thanks to you," I said sadly. "A relic of the past, like the elevated train and the *Live Poultry Fresh Killed* sign."

Holiday shook her head. "The *Live Poultry Fresh Killed* sign is still there," she reminded me.

"It's not," I said. The *Live Poultry Fresh Killed* sign had hung outside a wholesale butcher in Somerville for decades, an enormous yellow beacon for all of a person's dead-bird needs. "They sold the building and took it down. I think it went to auction."

Holiday looked deeply skeptical. "Are you sure?" she asked. "I'm pretty sure I drove past it like, sometime in the last year."

"You didn't," I said, "because it's not there anymore."

"Really?"

"Do you not believe me?"

"I kind of don't."

"Fine," I said, "let's get in your car right now and I will prove it to you."

"Fine," Holiday echoed, smirking at me. Her dark eyes were shining as she held a hand out so I could pull her to her feet. "Let's."

"We should wager something," I said as I got our jackets from the closet, dorkily excited. "You know, make it interesting."

Holiday stopped with her coat half-on. "Okay," she agreed slowly, her gaze even on mine. "What did you have in mind?"

There was something in her voice that had me thinking about the other night at the lax house. There was something in her voice that had me looking at her mouth.

That was when the bell rang again.

"Jesus, it's like South Station in here today," my mom said, coming in from the kitchen and pressing the intercom button. "Hello?"

"Um, hello?" crackled a voice on the other end. "I'm not sure I have the— Is this Linden's house? This is Greer."

"Oh!" my mom said. "Okay." She let go of the button. "Michael?"

"Yeah," I agreed, like she'd been asking if that was in fact what she'd named me. I was frozen, standing there in the living room. I couldn't make myself move at all.

Finally, Holiday blew a noisy breath out and brushed past me, pressing the intercom button herself. "He'll be right down!" She looked back at me, gesturing toward the door. "Well?" she said, and I couldn't read the expression on her face. "Go."

"I—" I looked at the door, at her, back at the door again. "Okay," I agreed. "I'll be right back."

I thundered down the stairs and flung the front door open. There was Greer on the other side of it in hunter-green galoshes, her hair in a long braid over one shoulder. "Hi," she said.

"*Hi.*" There was a shiny black Jeep idling behind her at the curb, Maggie Rogers faintly audible on the sound system. I could see Margot scrolling through her phone behind the wheel. "Um. How did you know where I live?"

Greer tilted her head, her quirked lips slick with cherry Chap-Stick. "That," she said archly, "is . . . not *quite* the welcome I was hoping for."

"No, that's not—I mean, I'm glad to see you," I backpedaled— laughing a little, stepping back to let her into our dingy foyer. There were phone books piled to one side of the door; some mysterious company kept dropping them off faster than we could toss them into the recycling. A snow shovel leaned against the pock-marked wall next to a crusty five-gallon bucket of ice melt, even though the first snow was still at least a month away. "I'm just . . . surprised, that's all. Hi," I said again. "For real."

"Hi for real." Greer smiled at that.

"How was Thanksgiving?"

"Oh, god, you don't want to know." She shook her head. "It's over, which is honestly the nicest thing I can say about it. Oh, and there was creamed corn."

"I actually kind of like creamed corn," I admitted.

"You would."

"Is that an insult?"

"Maybe." Greer shrugged. "Anyway," she said, "I didn't come here to talk to you about that. I came here because I think I might have . . . overreacted the other day. When I told you not to come to camp."

"Oh yeah?" That got my attention. "You might have, huh?"

"Yeah." She blew a breath out. "You were just trying to protect me, right?"

I thought about that for a moment. *Trying to protect her* was one way of looking at it, obviously. It was what I'd told her last weekend underneath the bleachers, and it wasn't like it wasn't true: I cared hugely about Greer. If somebody wanted to hurt her, I wanted to stop them. If somebody was coming after her, I sure as shit wanted to stand in their way. But truthfully, there was more to it than that, something I knew I'd never be able to explain to her or, maybe, to anyone: the deep satisfaction that came from following a trail of clues, turning over rocks, and shining light into dark places. Of figuring out who'd done what and why. It was hard to name what I felt, solving mysteries with Holiday. If it hadn't been entirely too humiliating to contemplate, the word I might have used was *alive*.

"Yeah," I agreed quietly. "I was just looking out for you."

"Okay." Greer shrugged. "Well. Anyway. Everyone else thinks you're fun and wants you to come to Maine with us, so."

"Shows how much they know."

That made her smile. "Just," she said—taking a step toward me so our hips were only barely touching, a chilly wind blowing in through the open front door and ghosting over the back of my neck. "Come."

I took a breath. "Okay," I said, then immediately thought of my mom and Holiday two floors up, Holiday already in her puffy parka. I thought of *Live Poultry Fresh Killed*. "Let me, um . . . I'll meet you in the car, okay? I just need a minute."

Greer looked at me a little suspiciously. "Who are you embarrassed of here, Linden?"

"What? Nobody," I said, though of course the real answer was all three of them, for completely different reasons, in completely different ways. "They're—I mean, my mom is probably going to give me a hard time for bailing, that's all."

Greer nodded slowly. "Well," she said, and tipped her face up to kiss me. "In that case, I will have to be sure to make it worth your while."

I grinned against her mouth. "I'll be right back."

"Uh-huh." She laid one chilly hand against the flat of my chest, then slid it down my body and squeezed. "I'll be here."

When I got back up to the apartment, Holiday was still wearing her coat, her tote bag slung over one shoulder. "Ready to go see the chicken sign?" she deadpanned. Then, off my presumably stricken face: "I'm kidding, dumbass. Go do your thing."

"I'm sorry," I said, scrubbing a hand through my hair. "I feel like a total dick."

"I mean, you *are* a total dick," Holiday said cheerfully, "but it's fine. Seriously, Michael, go have fun."

"Really?" Normally, I knew when Holiday was full of shit, but I couldn't get a read on her expression. It was disconcerting; she was a good actress, sure, but I wasn't used to her turning that particular skill on me. "Are you sure?"

"Yes!" She laughed—a little shrilly, maybe? I wasn't sure. "Dude," she said, "you obviously want to go. I *want* you to go."

"You want me to go, or you think I want to go?"

Holiday rolled her eyes. "I'm not doing this with you," she said. "Goodbye. See if you can find out anything about Emily, or who Greer was meeting the night of your accident. I'll talk to you in a few days."

"Okay," I agreed, unable to shake the creeping sense of unease in my chest and my stomach but not knowing what to do about it either. "A few days."

14

I KNEW FROM SPENDING THREE YEARS AT BARTLEY that there were certain words—*cabin, cottage, a little place on the Cape*—that didn't always mean what they seemed to, but still I was surprised by Margot's family's camp, which was just outside a small beach town in mid-coast Maine. The house looked like a fancy, rustic hotel, all amber light and craftsman architecture, leaded stained-glass windows; the wide front porch was lined with rocking chairs, a dozen of them in a row. It looked like the kind of place Teddy Roosevelt would have come to shoot pheasants.

There were ten of us, all told: Greer and Margot and me, Margot's cousins James and Tanner, plus Tanner's buddy Leo and a girlfriend of indeterminate provenance, a blond with a weirdly deep voice like a radio announcer. Celine and Dagny arrived after midnight, having driven all the way up from New York with Celine's weird boyfriend Henry in tow. In fact, the only one of the suitemates who *hadn't* joined was Keiko, and I reflexively wondered if there was a reason why before reminding myself it didn't matter. I hadn't come here to play detective—or if I had, that wasn't the main reason. I'd come here to be with Greer. And if there was a tiny part of me that couldn't help but think about what Holiday had said that day by the Charles River, about making the safe and unadventurous choice, I pushed it out of my mind. After all, I told myself as I helped James lift the lid off the enormous hot tub on the back deck overlooking the Atlantic, I'd known Holiday longer than anyone. Didn't that make my friendship with her the safest choice of all?

We spent Friday night getting drunk and playing pool under the warm yellow light in the library, a surprising flash in James's eyes when Tanner's friend Leo, who hadn't said more than three words since he'd gotten out of Tanner's Audi, beat him three times in a row. I didn't love James, his easy smile belying a canny sharpness to his gaze, a hidden hostility in the hang of his shoulders. *Not everyone is a suspect,* I heard Holiday tell me; still, from the way I heard James complaining to Margot in the butler's pantry that between her and Tanner they'd brought every stray dog in New England, I suspected he didn't love me either. "That dude, right?" I muttered to Leo, handing him a beer out of the fridge as James held forth in the dining room about the redundancy of original art in the age of artificial intelligence. Leo offered a small smile in return.

Saturday morning dawned gray and drizzly. We went on a long, winding hike after breakfast, the fog hanging densely in the air. Birds called to each other high in the bare trees, the trail covered with a thick carpet of half-rotted leaves. I could smell the ocean, though I couldn't see it, the crash of the waves faintly audible against the rocky shore.

Greer started out at the front of the group with Dagny, then gradually slowed her pace; I matched her, both of us falling back until we were far enough behind the group that we could talk in private. It felt like she was working up to something, and eventually she took a breath. "So," she said. "About last night, when I came to pick you up. That was Holiday's voice on the intercom, right?"

For a moment I considered lying, and I didn't want to think about why. "Yeah," I admitted. "She was there."

Greer nodded. "And when you opened the door . . . it kind of seemed like maybe you weren't that excited to see me."

"That's not true," I said immediately. "Greer, I was *dying* to see you. All semester, I've been dying to see you. Holiday is a family friend, that's all. I promise, there's nothing like that between us." I thought of that kiss in Hunter's room, then immediately stopped thinking about it. "And as for the other thing . . . I just get weird about my house, that's all. I wasn't expecting you to show up. You know how you're always supposed to wear clean underwear in case you get in a car accident and the paramedics see it? It's like that."

"Your house is dirty underwear?"

"My house is a two-bedroom apartment in an Eastie triple decker with like, Etsy cross-stitch on the walls," I said. "It's not like this, that's for sure." I shrugged. "I was . . . surprised."

Surprised wasn't the right word. In fact, I'd been mortified, like she'd caught me masturbating with Jell-O or reading X-rated Harry Styles fan fiction on Wattpad. Greer, like almost everyone else I'd known back at Bartley, came from a ton of money, and I could only imagine what the apartment would have looked like to her: our hand-me-down sofa and dinged-up coffee table, the lopsided afghans my mom liked to crochet while she watched TV at night. The people I'd gone to school with had Hockneys and Basquiats on display in their living rooms, not samplers that said *Fuck the Patriarchy* in cutesy pink script.

"I mean, for the record, my house isn't like this either," Greer pointed out now, "but I hear what you're saying." She bumped my shoulder with hers. "It's just me, Linden. We dated for like, almost a full year. I definitely wasn't expecting you to live in some giant mansion out in Groton or wherever the fuck. On top of which, I don't know what I've ever said that would make you think I give a shit about stuff like that."

"Nothing," I admitted truthfully. "You never did."

"Well then," she said pointedly. She was wearing a black cashmere sweater under her anorak, her eyes dark and serious behind the round frames of her glasses. "Relax."

"Was Thanksgiving really that bad?"

Greer wrinkled her nose. "My dad was all over me about my grades again," she said. "Which, like, my grades are actually pretty good this semester! I think, barring some kind of disaster, I am in fact going to pull myself out of academic probation purgatory. But it doesn't even matter to him, because I've got the stink on me now. I could finish out my academic career fucking summa cum laude and still all he would want to talk about in the toast at my graduation dinner would be the incomplete I got in biochem my first semester."

I frowned. "That sucks, Greer."

Greer shrugged, her shoulders jerking violently. "I mean, it could have been worse," she admitted after a moment. "My cousin Emily got in a knock-down drag-out fight with her mom during cocktail hour and wound up having her degenerate boyfriend pick her up halfway through dinner, though not before she took an entire tray of rolls off the table and dumped them ostentatiously into her purse, so." She smiled a little wistfully. "Probably nobody will even remember how disappointed my father is in me."

I worked very, very hard not to react. "That was considerate of her," I agreed carefully. I'd been trying to figure out a way to bring up Emily without Greer knowing I was fishing. "Emily, I mean."

"It was," Greer agreed, though she wasn't meeting my eyes. I sensed there was more to the story here, so I tried Holiday's trick of staying silent, and sure enough, after a moment Greer went on. "Em is only like, nine months younger than me," she said, ducking under a low-hanging evergreen branch. "We were like sisters when we were little kids—our moms dressed us the same for every holiday. Our parents would send us to our grandma's for four weeks every August. We called it Cousinland. We were obsessed with each other, basically. We were best friends. And then when we got to high school, all of that just . . . changed." She shrugged. "When we were sophomores she got this stupid boyfriend who was older—"

"Dinner rolls guy?" I asked, but Greer shook her head.

"Different guy than dinner rolls guy, but—not coincidentally—also a total dirtbag. And by the next time I saw her she was like, sneaking pills out of her parents' medicine cabinet, and the time after *that* she was fully high off her ass at the Fourth of July."

"Like Bri, you mean?"

Greer looked at me a little strangely. "Bri was a good time," she clarified, as though the difference should have been obvious. "Emily is an addict."

I *whoof*ed a breath out. "That sucks."

"It does suck."

A thought occurred to me. "The night of the accident—our accident," I said carefully. "When you said you had family stuff to take care of . . ."

"Yeah." Greer nodded. "She was home from Saint Paul's for spring break and owed some money to some scummy low-level dealer she knew. She called me to bail her out, so I did. She needed cash." She sighed. "It scared me, you know? Seeing her like that."

"It sounds scary," I said, remembering how tense she'd seemed that night, the way her hands had gripped the steering wheel of her car as we'd started to skid. "Greer—"

"I know what you're going to say." She cut me off, holding one manicured hand up to stop me. "That she's probably the one who took my watch, right? Some crummy addict who'd do anything for money? But Emily isn't like that, Linden." Greer's voice was emphatic. "She would never do anything to hurt me, and I don't want you to go back to sniffing around—"

"I wasn't going to say any of that," I said, which was true, though I had a hundred percent been thinking it. More than that, I was thinking that Emily very well might have killed Bri. After all, I'd seen her in Hemlock House the day Greer's room was ransacked. What if she'd come back the night of the Halloween party to see if she'd missed anything, and Bri had caught her in the act? "And I'm not going to—what did you say?—*sniff around* anybody.

I was actually just going to ask why you never told me about her back at Bartley."

Greer shrugged, her body language relaxing a little. "I guess I wasn't sure you were the real deal," she said softly. "Or, like—that *we* were the real deal."

"And now?"

Greer stopped walking then. She wrapped her arms around my neck and tilted her face up, pressing her mouth against mine while a bird called out somewhere high in the tops of the pine trees. "You tell me."

I kissed her, pulling her even closer; she stumbled a little, her body pressing warmly against mine. All at once I didn't care about Emily, or Bri, or Holiday. All I wanted was to keep on kissing Greer. "Can I tell you something?" I said, even as she curled her hands into my jacket to keep her balance. "I've never really liked hiking that much anyway."

Greer kept her eyes locked on mine. "How about that," she said, the intent in her grin unmistakable. "Me either."

Greer shot a quick text to Margot so she wouldn't worry we were lost in the woods somewhere, and we turned around and hurried back down the trail the same way we'd come, letting ourselves into the dim, quiet house. Empty, the place gave off kind of a haunted vibe, with its stained-glass windows and its antique rugs, but I only had a second to think about it before Greer was pulling me toward the bedroom we were sharing, her dark hair crackling with static electricity in the cold, dry cabin air. "You coming?" she asked, looking back at me over one shoulder. I nodded and followed her upstairs.

15

THE OTHERS STOPPED OFF AFTER THEIR HIKE AT SOME Maine dive bar that didn't card, and it was near dark by the time they got back to the house in a cacophony of chatter. "Cavalry's coming," Greer said, nudging her knee against mine under the covers; we got dressed as quickly as we could and joined them downstairs, where Margot was opening what looked like a very fancy bottle of red wine. "Oh, *hello* there!" she trilled, popping the cork with a flourish. "You guys enjoy your afternoon?"

I could feel myself blush, but Greer just smiled. "We did, in fact. Thank you for asking." She plucked a wineglass from the rack. "How was the rest of the hike?"

We spent the next couple of hours getting cheerily drunk, James and his buddy Leo posting up at the pool table while Greer held court in an enormous leather recliner and Dagny and Margot painstakingly re-created a dance from some Disney Channel movie they'd both liked as kids. "Linden!" Margot ordered, yanking her phone out of her leggings pocket and waving it in my direction without missing a step. "Come here, take a video."

I grabbed her phone and dutifully opened the camera app; I was just about to hit record when a text popped up from a contact listed in Margot's phone as Boy Genius. *Not to be that person, but we still need to deal with the Greer situation.* Then, half a second later: *I know you don't want to think about it, but if she runs her mouth we're fucked.*

Holy *shit.* I froze for a second, then glanced around wildly, but the rest of the group had drifted out onto the deck. "Did you take it?" Margot asked, looking at me a little oddly.

"Um," I said. "Sorry, I had it on portrait. Try again?"

"I remember the first time I used a cell phone," Greer heckled me from across the room, her cheeks flushed a winning pink from the wine.

"Yeah, yeah." I tucked the text—and the question of who the hell Boy Genius might be—into the back of my head for later consideration. "Okay, go."

Margot was the kind of girl who liked playing hostess, who you could tell was going to grow up to throw elaborate dinner parties involving oysters and cheesecloth. That night she took the better part of three hours to prepare an Italian-style feast she'd found on TikTok, using what had to be every dish and pan in the professionally outfitted kitchen, only to wrinkle her nose in disgust upon taking her first bite of pasta. "This," she announced brightly, "is . . . inedible."

"It's not!" Greer promised, though in fact it sort of was—gluey and garlic-forward, already mostly cold. "It's good."

"It's pretty bad," Celine put in helpfully.

"Fuck you," Margot said sweetly, "and fuck dinner. We're skipping to dessert." She disappeared into the kitchen and came back with a box wrapped in gold ribbon. Inside were a dozen intricately decorated truffles, each one nestled in a fluted paper cup.

"A guy I know in town makes these," Margot explained as she passed them around the table; from the way she said it she could have meant some bespoke chocolatier in suspenders just as easily as some dude who sold Gatorades at the gas station and had a little hustle on the side. "He said they're the real deal, so one per customer, please, children. The closest hospital is like forty minutes away."

"Here," Greer said, handing me the box. I only hesitated for a second before popping one into my mouth. It was more bitter than I was expecting, a little unpleasant. All at once it occurred to me that maybe I should have asked a question or two before tossing it down the hatch.

Once she'd finished her own truffle, Margot nodded at James across the table. "Okay," she said with a businesslike clap of her hands, "are we ready to play?"

"Play what?" I asked, suddenly suspicious.

"Catch the Turkey," Greer said with a roll of her eyes.

"What's Catch the Turkey?"

"Pretty much exactly what it says on the label." James grinned from down the table. "We take him out into the woods, set him free, give him a head start. First one to catch him wins."

"Wait," I said, momentarily confused. I really, *really* did not want to accidentally participate in any more animal cruelty this semester. "Like, an actual turkey?"

Margot laughed. "No, sweet pea," she said, like it should have been obvious. "Not an actual turkey."

I shook my head. "Then who—?"

"FNG," James announced. "It's only fair."

"FNG?" Celine asked.

"Fuckin' new guy," I said quietly, a slow, sick feeling of dread settling over me. I'd been the fuckin' new guy enough in my life that I answered to it almost instinctively, which was why I was so surprised when James turned to Leo instead.

"Sorry, old chum," he said, reaching over and squeezing one of Leo's skinny shoulders. "Look like you're it tonight."

"Fuck you, James," Leo said, but he didn't quite stick the landing.

"James—" Tanner started, then broke off as soon as James raised his eyebrows; all at once I thought I probably understood everything I needed to about the intricacies of that particular fraternal relationship. I'd known people like James before, the way privilege can burnish a person to a shine so glossy it's easy to miss the mean streak. I'd known people like Tanner too.

"What happens when you catch him?" I asked.

"That," James said lightly, "is up to whoever does the catching."

"Anyway, that's not the point." Margot's smile was luminous. "The thrill is the chase."

"Are you serious?" I shook my head. "That doesn't feel like, kind of fucked up to you?"

"Spoken like a guy who wants to be the turkey," Henry said.

"Shut up, Henry," Dagny said, reaching for her wineglass. "I don't want any part of this, for the record. I'm going to go be high in the hot tub like God intended and you all can come find me when you're done."

"Yeah," I heard myself say, looking down the table at Leo, whose pale cheeks were flushed bright red. "Bro, you definitely don't have to—"

"It's fine, dude." I recognized the way Leo raised his chin, like he was daring James to punch him. Like he was daring *me* to. "I can handle it."

"I'm not saying you can't *handle* it, I just think it's—" I turned to Greer. "Are you doing this?" I asked her.

Greer shrugged. "It's just a game, Linden," she said softly. "It's supposed to be fun."

"And you've played it before?"

"Pal, it's essentially tag," James said, sitting back in his seat and fixing me with a gaze of benign contempt. "Are you really going to be a little pissant about a game of tag?"

And: no.

In the end, I suppose I wasn't.

Out on the front porch Margot blew a tiny whistle, all of us scattering into the darkness of the woods beyond the circle of outbuildings—one, Margot had explained with a wryness that might or might not have been the genuine article, for each branch of the family tree—that ringed the main house. It was freezing, the winds screaming through the pine trees overhead. The place felt haunted, which I knew in some part of my brain wasn't possible but which felt all at once like the only logical conclusion; I thought of bears and wolves and owls with talons big enough to carry a grown man off into the darkness. I thought of ghosts wandering sorrowfully through the trees.

I blinked, trying to orient myself, but my brain was as foggy as the trail had been earlier that day, everything taking on a hazy sheen and a low buzz humming at the back of my head. When I'd eaten the chocolate I'd figured it was weed; shit like that was almost always weed, as far as I knew. But all at once I realized it hadn't been—or at least, if it *had* been, it wasn't like any weed I'd ever had before.

I was fully prepared to wander the woods forever, licking dewdrops off leaves to stay alive, when the glowing yellow lights of the main house rose before me. I ran out of the woods like I was being chased, then stumbled through the door and up the stairs into the bathroom before collapsing onto the floor and pressing my cheek against the black and white hexagonal tiles with the unshakeable certainty that I would always be high, I would never *not* be high, I would be high until the day many years from now when I died, presumably from the stress put on my body from still being high. It was nice down here, actually. The floors were so clean I could have eaten Thanksgiving dinner off them. Maybe I could just stay down here forever. That might not be so bad.

At last I dug my phone out of my jeans pocket, closing one eye to try to see the screen clearly. I thought again of the text Boy Genius had sent to Margot: *If she runs her mouth we're fucked.* I thought of what Greer had told me about Emily on our hike, and of Holiday's face in my living room right before I'd left the apartment yesterday, the dark inscrutability of her expression. Then I opened my recent contacts and scrolled to her name.

I was expecting her to answer right away—one thing about Holiday was that she always had her phone on her—but it rang for a long time before she finally picked up. "Hi!" she said cheerfully, and it felt like putting aloe on a sunburn before the outgoing voice mail message continued. "You've reached Holiday Proctor. If you get this message, hang up and send me a text. Not you, Bubbe, you're good. I'll call you back as soon as I can."

"It's me," I said after the beep, squeezing my eyes shut; I knew there had definitely been times in my life when I'd felt lonelier than I did in that moment, but I couldn't think of any off the top of my head. "I guess you're out. Or sleeping, maybe. It might be late. I took an edible, but I think it might have been like . . . laced with something? Or maybe that's just how edibles are. I've never done edibles before. I'm not really a drug guy. Although I guess alcohol is a drug, right? It's a . . . depressant." I blinked, scrubbing a hand over my face. "I'm at Margot's, did I say that already? Or I guess you . . . know that.

"Anyway," I continued, "they had us play this fucked-up game where we had to chase a turkey. Not a real turkey. I don't want you to think I'm not a supporter of animal rights, what with the whole goldfish thing. Pattern of behavior, I know." I could tell even in the moment that I wasn't making sense. "Anyway. I do actually have a reason for calling." I filled her in on the message I'd seen on Margot's phone—at least, I tried to—plus an abbreviated version of the story Greer had told me about Emily. "Anyway," I said again, "both of those could be something, right? Or maybe nothing. It's

kind of weird here. I probably should have just stayed, yesterday."
I sighed. "I'm sorry. I keep thinking about kissing you."

Oh, *fuck.*

The floor tilted under me then, even though I was already lying
down. "I *mean*," I said, trying to push myself upright—trying to
recover but not able to quite make it happen, "just that I probably
shouldn't have done it. Not that I like, regret it or anything. Just
that, um. Like. You're my best friend, obviously. And that's not
really . . . a thing it's cool for best friends to do. Maybe in France.
Or like, some of the girls at Bartley used to, but that was kind of a
different—" I broke off. "I should go. Okay. Call me back. Or not,
if you're busy. Tell your bubbe hello for me."

It took me three tries to end the call, my finger slipping uselessly against the smudgy screen of my phone. Once it finally went
dark I laid my head back down on the tile, closing my eyes against
the spinning and waiting for a morning that felt a million years
away.

16

WHEN I WOKE UP IT WAS DECEMBER, AND SOMEONE was pissing enthusiastically into the toilet beside me. "Don't mind me," James said, his voice cheerful as I blinked rapidly, hideously alert. "Didn't mean to startle you."

"Dude," I managed, scrubbing a hand over my swollen, throbbing face, "there are like, twelve bathrooms in this house."

"Emergency," he said pleasantly. His pajama pants were printed with tiny red lobsters. "Couldn't wait. Honestly, all things considered, you're lucky all I had to do was pee."

I winced, waiting until he was finished washing his hands before I pushed myself cautiously upright. I was still wearing my clothes from the night before, the smell of wood and bonfire smoke wafting off me every time I moved. My joints ached. My mouth felt cottony. And I was filled with the kind of sticky black dread that oozes into every cranny and crevice, a sick certainty that some grave disaster was coming and I was its unlucky author. I could only remember bits and pieces of anything that had happened once Leo had taken off into the woods—the weirdness with Greer, the breathing trees, and—*woof*—the message I'd left for Holiday. What had I even *said*? The whole thing was hazy, but judging by the creeping, moldy feeling in my chest, it couldn't have been—

I keep thinking about kissing you.

Oh, fuck me.

"Bro," James said, glancing at me over his shoulder as he headed into the hallway, "you gonna boot?"

"No," I said, gripping the edge of the bathtub and waiting for him to go away. "I'm good."

Once I was finally alone I dug my phone out of my pocket with shaking hands, hoping maybe I'd hallucinated the whole thing, but there it was: *outgoing call, 4 minutes, 11:17 p.m.* I had no idea if she'd gotten it already; she hadn't called me back, or even texted. I swiped over to our message thread, my thumb flying: *So, hey. Lots to fill you in on. Back tonight, but in the meantime, if you've got a long voice mail from me you haven't listened to yet . . . maybe don't?*

I followed up a second later: *I realize that me saying that is probably just going to make you want to listen immediately, but. Really. Better to delete.* Then, most pathetic of all, I tried one more time: *lol.*

I waited for a minute to see if she'd text back, which she didn't, then shoved my phone into my pocket with a grumble and shuffled downstairs to the kitchen, where I found Greer sitting at the long farmhouse table with Margot and Celine and Dagny, all of them eating sticky buns as big as their heads.

"There you are," Greer said, pulling off one long, gooey piece and popping it into her mouth. "I was going to come poke you in a minute to make sure you were alive." She looked at me, presumably taking in my pale, sweaty face. "There's coffee."

"Thank you." I poured a cup from the fancy machine, willing myself to steady out. The dull panic coursing through my body felt worse than just normal morning-after anxiety, a kind of foreboding I couldn't shake. I didn't know if it was the aftereffects of whatever had been in the edibles or just the catastrophe of my own bad judgment. "I passed out on the bathroom floor."

"I know," she said, not unkindly. "I tried to move you when we got back into the house. You told me to go away and that you were communing with the tile."

"I mean, it is very lovely tile," Dagny agreed, barely holding in her laughter as she patted the bench beside her. "Come have a sticky bun."

It was already close to noon, and Margot needed to get back to campus to work on a group project, so once I'd finished my coffee we all headed upstairs to pack. "What are you doing?" Margot asked when she saw me hauling an armload of bedding down the back stairs.

I froze. "Bringing the sheets down?" I explained, feeling a little bit sheepish. "I was gonna throw them into the machine."

Margot's lips quirked. "You definitely don't need to do that."

"I don't mind," I said. I looked around at the kitchen, taking in the mess on the counters, the muddy boot prints by the door. The trash was piled high in the stainless steel can. "We should probably clean up a little before we go, right?"

Margot shook her head. "It's fine," she promised. "The housekeeper will be here this afternoon. She'll take care of it."

The housekeeper. I glanced out the window at the fine wash of sleet coming down on the driveway, thought of my mom spending a snowy Sunday schlepping the vacuum up the grand front steps. "Okay," I said uneasily. "Well, as long as I'm down here, I might as well toss them in."

Margot shrugged. "Sure," she said, "suit yourself."

So I ran a load of laundry, carried Greer's bag down to the Jeep. "Oh, shit," I said as we were hauling the last of our stuff into the trunk, "I think I left my hoodie upstairs." I doubled back into the house and tidied up the kitchen as fast as I could, starting the dishwasher and tying up the trash bags before digging all the cash I had out of my wallet and leaving it on the kitchen table on top of a paper towel, scrawling *housekeeping* across it with a pen I found in a drawer. "Where's the hoodie?" Greer asked when I climbed into the Jeep a few minutes later, breathing a little hard.

"I realized I already packed it," I said. "I'm a dumbass."

"Only sometimes," she replied, scooting over in the back seat to make room.

It felt like the ride back to Boston took forever, the stop-and-start of the Thanksgiving weekend traffic making me queasy. Since the accident I could be a little weird about driving in bad weather, especially with people I didn't know that well. "You okay?" Greer murmured as Margot flipped off a minivan behind her on 95 South. "You look like you're about to pass out."

"Just hungover," I said, which was partly true. "Which reminds me: What happened with the, ah, turkey?"

Both of them burst out laughing at that.

When we got back to campus I basically tucked and rolled out of the car, saying a hurried goodbye to the girls outside of Hemlock and dialing Holiday's number as I darted up the stairs of my dorm. "So, I'm guessing you got my other message," I said when she sent me to voice mail one more time. "Like I said in my text this morning, definitely feel free to just ignore that, but—"

I broke off as I opened the door to my room—and found Holiday cross-legged on my mattress eating a paper cup of ice cream from J.P. Licks. Duncan was sitting in his desk chair opposite, his feet propped up on the bed. I blinked, looking from Holiday to Duncan and back to Holiday again. "Are you waiting for me?" I asked her.

"Always," Holiday deadpanned, then rolled her eyes. "No, Michael." She nodded at Duncan—who, I saw now, had his own cup of ice cream. They'd been hanging out here, I realized belatedly. In my room. *Together.*

On *purpose.*

"Dave's connecting flight is delayed in Chicago," Duncan reported cheerfully, his ruddy hair flopping down over his forehead. "How was your break?"

"It was good," I said absently, still trying to tease out exactly how this scene before me had come into existence. Who ate ice cream in December, anyway? It was unnatural.

Holiday scraped the bottom of her cup with her plastic spoon. "I should get going," she announced, tossing them into the trash can underneath my desk. "Duncan, I'll text you about the—"

"The reading at Trident," he finished for her. "Yeah, definitely."

"It's a date."

A *date*? My head banged. Fuck, at this rate I was going to be hungover until New Year's. "I can walk you down," I managed. I was still wearing my coat, suddenly sweating in the overwarm residence hall.

Holiday shook her head. "I'm good," she said, but I followed her anyway, trailing her down the hallway and onto the staircase.

"Hey," I said. "So, about that message—"

"Don't worry about it," she said airily, holding a hand up in an attempt, presumably, to save me from myself. "I could only understand, like, half of what you were saying anyway. Who's Boy Genius?"

"I have no idea," I said. "But I think it's worth looking into, right? If Greer somehow found out something incriminating about him and Margot—"

"Trying to shut her up could be enough of a motive for them to come after her," Holiday admitted. "It probably makes sense to put eyes on Margot for a couple of days, see if she leads us anywhere interesting."

I nodded. "And Emily? It seems weird that Greer didn't mention her being on campus the day her room got trashed, right?"

"Yeah." Holiday sighed. "Can you please do me a favor and try to figure out what Greer's mom's maiden name is?" she asked. "I mean, I'm a pretty good internet detective, but there are thirty-two thousand students at BU and like four thousand of them are named Emily."

"Yeah, of course," I promised. It occurred to me that she didn't sound particularly enthusiastic about the idea; I wondered if the novelty of this particular investigation was starting to wear off for her, though it could have just been that my head was still pounding and all my joints kind of hurt. "I'm happy to help." Then, because I couldn't quite stop myself: "So you and Duncan, huh?"

Holiday made a face and shoved her hands into her coat pockets at the same time she shrugged, a Thanksgiving cornucopia of nervous body language. "It's not a big deal," she said. "We've been talking a little bit, that's all."

I raised an eyebrow. "So I see."

"He couldn't afford to fly home just for the weekend," she continued as she got to the bottom of the stairs and opened the door to the bustling lobby. "He's on scholarship, just like you."

I blinked. "He is?" I hadn't known that; I'd never thought to ask about his plans. It made me feel like a dick in a way I didn't want to examine too closely.

"He is," she reported. "Imagine that." She pushed open the door of the building, an icy blast of wind blowing through. "I'll talk to you tomorrow, Michael," she told me. "Meanwhile, drink some water, will you? You look like you're about to keel over and die."

"Thanks for that."

"Anytime."

Once she was gone I headed back upstairs to my room, where Duncan had finished his ice cream and was stretched out in bed with a chemistry book. "Hey, dude," I said, reaching out and running a hand over my bedspread, smoothing out the place where Holiday had been. "I think I owe you an apology."

17

Thursday, 12/5/24

"MY BACK HURTS," I COMPLAINED ON THURSDAY AFTER-
noon, crouched on the fourth-floor landing of the dimly lit stairwell at Hemlock House. "Remind me again why we can't just wait
outside the building?"

"It's suspicious," Holiday countered. She was close enough that
I could smell the faint Earl Grey smell of her, her neck craned so
she could peer out the narrow window in the staircase door. "Also,
it's thirty degrees."

"How is it suspicious?" I asked. "I literally go to this college."

"I don't," Holiday reminded me. "And neither one of us lives
here. Do you really want to have to explain to Greer what you and
I were doing lurking around outside her dorm room like a couple
of weirdos?"

"Waiting to surprise her with a candygram," I posited, only
half joking. "Looking for my lost contact lens."

Holiday made a face. Both of us were punchy and bored; we'd
spent the better part of the last three days tailing Margot around

campus—or, more accurately, *I* had spent the better part of the last three days tailing Margot around campus, with Holiday dropping in for backup whenever she could—and so far it had been the dullest and most uneventful stakeout in the history of all humankind. We'd watched as Margot went to the library and worked on a paper. I'd followed her to a yoga class at the gym. We'd seen her buy a blueberry fig bar at the convenience store, then double back for a bottle of fizzy water; it was scintillating stuff, truly, but none of it had given us any indication of who Boy Genius might be, or what secret he and Margot might have been protecting from Greer. My neck ached. I had homework I should have been doing. And I was feeling more than a little like a dumbass.

"This is a waste of time," I declared.

"Maybe," Holiday agreed amiably. "You want to quit?"

I sighed. "No," I admitted. "But I would feel better if we'd been able to find anything on Emily so we could at least be sure we're even focusing on the right lead." An obituary for Greer's paternal grandpa in the *New Haven Register* had led us to her parents' marriage announcement; assuming Emily was related on Greer's mom's side, her last name was possibly Hawker, but a search of that name hadn't turned up anything useful.

"I wish I could figure out where I recognized her from," Holiday said, running her hands through her wild mass of curly hair. "It's driving me out of my mind."

"Senior citizens' water aerobics?" I teased, naming an actual class Holiday had taken at the Cambridge Y over the summer.

"Nah, it was probably leg day with my bros at the gym," she shot back.

"Rager at the lax house, maybe?" I asked—then, realizing it was a little too close to the thing we weren't talking about, I cleared my throat. "So," I said, glancing out the door of the stairwell one more time, "you and Duncan."

Holiday snorted. "What about me and Duncan?"

"Are you guys, like, dating now? Is it serious? Should I expect to come home and find a sock on the—"

"Easy, tiger." Holiday cut me off. "I like him," she admitted. "I mean, I don't know that we're going to be spending New Year's Eve together or anything, but I'm willing to see how it goes."

"Is that your measurement of a relationship with promise?" I teased, rolling my shoulders to ease the cramp there. "New Year's Eve plans?"

"Yes," Holiday said immediately. Then, at my dubious expression: "I mean, think about it. In terms of significant calendar dates, New Year's is a bigger deal than Valentine's Day. It's more important than your birthday, even. By spending New Year's Eve with someone, you're basically saying, *I want to be with you in the past and in the future. I want to sit with you in the tension between the old world and the new one. I want to be with you for all time.*"

"I mean, sure, I guess." I blinked at the intensity of it. "Or, alternately: *I want to get drunk with you at a party and watch for cars while you pee on the curb at three a.m.*"

Holiday rolled her eyes. "It's truly a wonder that publishers aren't clamoring at the door for your collection of original love poetry."

"I'm an undiscovered talent," I agreed. Holiday and I had spent at least three or four New Year's Eves together in elementary and middle school, actually, eating popcorn at her parents' house and staying up to watch the ball drop, though neither one of us mentioned that now. We'd been kids, that was all. She wasn't talking about when you were kids. "Is that what happened with Evan?" I asked, picking at my cuticles instead of looking directly at her. "You didn't want to spend New Year's Eve with him? You never really said."

Holiday glanced at me sidelong. "No," she agreed, her voice clipped. "I guess I didn't."

"So?" I prompted.

"So what, exactly?"

"I mean, nothing." I wasn't sure why she was being so evasive all of a sudden, but if there was one thing she'd taught me, it was that the questions people wanted to avoid were usually the ones worth pursuing. "Just wanted to know if you needed me to beat him up, that's all."

Holiday snorted. "Why do you assume he broke up with me?" she asked. "For all you know, I could have been the one who ended it."

"Were you?"

"No," she admitted, leaning her head back against the wall. "He was. But I could have been."

"Did he give you a reason?"

"Does it matter?"

"I—" I broke off, trying to think how to answer that. "Yes," I said eventually, which was the truth even if I didn't totally understand why.

Holiday looked at me for a long moment. Then she sighed. "He said I wasn't in it," she reported flatly.

"Meaning . . ."

"We got in this stupid fight," she said, leaning her head back against the wall. "He was going to backpack through Europe for all of June and July, and he wanted me to go with him."

I blinked. "Wow." Holiday and I had spent the entire summer together, eating ice cream from Christina's and watching the entirety of a sleepy PBS show she liked about a British veterinarian. She'd never mentioned she could have been sipping champagne at a café overlooking the Eiffel Tower and looking at artifacts stolen from colonized nations, or whatever people did on vacation abroad. "And you didn't want to?"

"First of all," Holiday said, "do I look to you for one second like a person who would enjoy backpacking anywhere? I don't even like backpacking to *school.*" She shook her head. "But also, it was my last summer before college, you know? I just . . . wanted to spend it here." She shrugged. "Anyway, then it turned into this whole big thing about how he loved me more than I loved him and how I'd had one foot out the door ever since we started dating, like I was just biding my time waiting for—" She broke off. "Whatever. Something better to come along."

"Were you?" I asked, the words coming out a little more quickly than I'd meant for them to.

Holiday shrugged one more time. "Maybe. I don't know." She crossed her arms. "I don't want to talk about this anymore, Michael."

"Why n—"

Holiday grabbed my elbow before I could get the question out, lifting her chin in the direction of the suite: Margot was headed down the hall toward the elevator, dressed in a puffy coat and a beanie, purse slung crosswise over her shoulder.

"Shit," Holiday hissed. "There she goes."

We scrambled to our feet, hustling down the stairs and bursting into the lobby just in time to see Margot disappear out the front door of Hemlock House. "This way," Holiday said quietly, nodding at the side entrance.

We followed her at a distance through the Square and down into the T station, then inbound to Park Street, where she transferred to the Green Line toward Allston. "Are we going to BU?" Holiday asked as the train shrieked out of the tunnel and onto the aboveground trolley tracks, craning her neck to try to keep eyes on Margot in the next car down. "I wonder if she's going to meet Emily. Is there a universe in which *Emily* is Boy Genius?" She frowned. "We should have brought disguises."

"Sox hats and fake mustaches," I agreed distractedly, peering over a businessman's shoulder.

"Large Dunkin' iced coffees."

"I would love a large Dunkin' iced coffee right now, actually."

"You know you might as well be paying four dollars for a plastic cup of water with a little dust sprinkled in."

"Also, cream and sugar—She's getting off," I interrupted myself, nodding as Margot stepped off the train and onto the platform. Holiday and I nearly took out a couple of old ladies in our hurry to follow, watching as Margot broke into a grin and waved at someone across the street. She darted through the traffic on Comm Ave, flinging herself with wild abandon directly into the arms of—

"Oh, fuck me," I said, stopping so short that Holiday crashed directly into my back.

"Who is that?" she hissed, peering over my shoulder. "The guy she's kissing?"

"That's James," I said. "Margot's cousin."

"Shut the fuck up," Holiday said, smacking me in the arm like I was joking, which I was emphatically not. Across the street Margot had popped up onto her tiptoes, her body pressed against James's right there in the middle of the sidewalk. "Are you sure they're real cousins? Maybe it's like one of those things where they're family friends but they call each other—"

"They're real cousins," I said grimly. "They were talking about their mean grandma when we were in Maine."

"Well, then maybe it's a WASP thing I just don't know about?" she asked hopefully.

"Tongue kissing your blood relative by way of greeting?"

"Whatever," Holiday said, a little defensive. "I don't know your fucking Wonder Bread customs. The point is—"

"The *point* is, we gotta tell Greer." I pulled my phone out of my jacket pocket. "Will you come with me to talk to her? I can have her meet us at my room."

"Hang on," Holiday said, holding a hand up. "Wait a second."

I paused, but only for a second, still scrolling to Greer's name in my contacts. "Why?"

"Because we don't *know* anything yet, Michael."

That stopped me. "What do you mean we don't know anything?" I gaped at her. "Why do you keep trying to slow this whole thing down?"

"I'm not trying to slow anything down," Holiday argued. "I'm trying to keep us—or, more specifically, I'm trying to keep *you*—from showing your ass to everyone in the entire commonwealth."

"I can cover my own ass," I snapped, more loudly than I meant to, then stopped and scrubbed a hand over my face. "Look," I tried. "We know Margot and James are hooking up, which means James is Boy Genius. We know Greer is onto them, which would give them motive. And Margot wasn't at the lacrosse party."

Holiday looked deeply skeptical. "What about the note, then?" she asked. "*You owe me*?"

"Maybe Margot wrote it to try to intimidate Greer into keeping quiet," I suggested. "Or maybe it's completely unrelated."

"Maybe," Holiday said, clearly unconvinced.

I sighed. "The point is, if we just went and *asked* Greer about it instead of sneaking around behind her back, she could tell us—"

"Greer has already been super clear that she thinks this whole thing is a shit show," Holiday argued. "Bringing her in now is just going to ruin the entire investigation."

"It's not going to ruin— Can I ask you something? What is it about Greer that bothers you so much?"

"Aaaand I'm going to stop you right there," Holiday declared, eyes narrowing. "You know what, Michael? Do whatever you want. We all know that's what you're doing to do anyway." She yanked her phone out of her coat pocket, glancing down at the screen. "I have to get back," she announced snottily. "Duncan's coming with me to a ballet thing at the Majestic."

"Oh, right." There was no reason for that to piss me off so much. "I forgot what a lover of ballet he is. Patron of the arts, truly."

Holiday gaped at me. "Oh, my god," she announced. "Oh, my god!" She put her hands on her face and made a big show of pulling her cheeks down, like the strain of talking to me was causing the flesh to melt right off her bones. "Why are you being like this?"

Uh-oh. Danger, Will Robinson. "Like what?" I asked—stalling, playing like I didn't know what she meant. At the very least I wanted to make her say it first.

Holiday wasn't having it. "Uh-uh," she said, holding a finger up. "You know like what."

"I really don't."

"Like you're four years old and he's playing with your trains and you don't like it."

"My trains, in this analogy, being you?"

Holiday blushed, which was the point. "That's not—" She shook her head. "I can't do this with you anymore, Michael."

"Can't do what?"

"Can't do any of it!" She whirled on me. "Why didn't you come to my showcase?"

I blinked. "Wha—"

"I told you about it, the night we went to South Street. You said you'd be there."

She had, I realized, with the sick, panicky feeling you get in a dream about sleeping through an important test, that warm wash of horror from your chest to your feet. She had told me about it—and not only had I forgotten to show up for it, I'd never even asked her how it went. All at once I remembered the night we'd gone to the party at the lax house, how quiet she'd seemed on the walk over: *Did something happen last night?* Something *had* happened. I'd flaked on her fucking show. "Shit, Holiday," I said. "I'm sorry. Why didn't you remind me?"

"First of all, I talked about rehearsals pretty much constantly," Holiday retorted. "And second of all, why does it have to be my job to remind you? Like, why do I have to do the emotional labor of constantly reminding you of every commitment you've ever made to me?"

"You said it wasn't a big deal!"

"And you *believed* me?" She made a face, and I didn't blame her. "Of course it was a big deal! Look, Michael, I don't know how to tell you this without sounding like an asshole, but I'm kind of like, doing some pretty cool shit for a freshman over at my school. And I can't even enjoy it because I'm always on the other side of the river traipsing through some garbage pile with you. And for what?"

"Nobody's forcing you to do any of this, Holiday." My face felt like it was on fire. "Excuse me for thinking we were friends, I guess."

"Friends?" Holiday echoed, barking out a sharp little laugh. "You think we're friends."

I frowned. "What are you— Of course we're friends."

Holiday planted her feet. "Who's my roommate, Michael?"

"What?"

"My roommate. At college. What's her name?"

I opened my mouth, then closed it again, racking my memory for some identifying detail. She must have mentioned it at some point. Chiara? Liz?

Holiday watched me wriggle for a moment before she finally shook her head. "I can see you're trying to remember," she said. "But it's not in your brain. I've never told you, because you've never asked. You've never asked about my roommate, or what classes I'm taking, or if I even like my program. For all you know I've dropped out of theater school entirely to study business at Northeastern, hoping to get a job selling mortgages when I graduate."

"I mean," I said. "At the very least, I'm pretty sure that's not true."

Holiday blew out a noisy breath. "The point is, if we were actually friends, all that stuff would have come up naturally in conversation. But it hasn't, because we're not. We're *not*!" It came out almost like a wail. "I'm just . . . a person who helps you solve shit. I'm like an extremely useful piece of office equipment to you. I'm an iPhone, but with breasts and an encyclopedic knowledge of the work of Stephen Sondheim."

"I ask you questions," I protested. "I asked you about why you and Evan broke up literally like two hours ago."

"Oh, well, in that case," Holiday scoffed. "One question about my failed relationship six months after the fact makes up for all the rest of it, I guess."

I didn't know how to respond to that, exactly. It felt like wading into a swamp filled with alligators. "We've been distracted," I said finally. "The start of freshman year, not to mention everything else that's been going on—"

But Holiday wasn't buying. "I would have shown up for you," she says. "I *always* show up for you. And I can't keep doing it, telling myself it's fine, that we have fun together, that it's enough. Like, just hanging around some college I don't even go to, waiting for you to suddenly—" She broke off, her expression stricken.

"Waiting for me to what?" My voice was very quiet.

"Forget it."

"Waiting for me to *what*, Holiday?" It felt like I was at the top of a tall building with no guardrails, looking over the edge a hundred stories down.

Holiday shook her head. "To wake up one day and suddenly be the kind of friend that I deserve."

"Bullshit," I told her flatly. "That's not what you were going to say. And it's the second time today you've started a sentence like that and then refused to finish it, so I don't think you're really in a position to be telling me what kind of interest I take or don't take in your—"

"See, this is why I didn't want to talk to you about this." Holiday cut me off, eyes flashing. "Because your ego is so fragile that like, any kind of feedback—"

"*Feedback?*" I echoed. "Is that what you call what's happening right now?"

"I'm not even saying anything mean, Michael! On top of which, I'm not even saying anything *new*. Our whole lives, our entire friendship has been on your terms."

"On *my* terms? You are unequivocally the boss of me, Holiday."

"If you think that, you're even stupider than you look."

Oh, I didn't like that. "Maybe we shouldn't be hanging out so much, then. You said it yourself, right? This is a city full of new people. Maybe both of us could stand to go meet some."

Holiday pressed her full lips together. I hadn't seen her cry in almost a decade, and for a second it almost looked like she was about to, but in the end she only lifted her chin like a queen. "Maybe we could," she agreed. "I'll see you around, Michael."

"Great," I agreed. "See you around."

18

THE PROBLEM WITH HAVING A KNOCK-DOWN, DRAG-out, friendship-ending fight with someone at the BU East stop on the Green Line when you live downtown and in Harvard Square, respectively: it makes storming off kind of a nonstarter. Holiday and I waited at opposite ends of the platform for the train to come, but when it finally chugged into sight it was only a single trolley car long, and enormously crowded. The front door was the only one to open.

I sighed noisily and shuffled into line behind her, getting a whiff of her hair for my trouble as I tapped my card and smushed myself into the three square inches of available standing room. Holiday didn't say anything, so I didn't either; both of us seethed in silence for ten excruciating stops until finally we got to Park Street and I shoved my way off. When I looked back through the window, I couldn't find her in the crush of commuters.

A bunch of guys from the lax team had gotten tickets to the Celtics game that evening, but I wasn't in the mood to hang out with anyone. Instead, I spent the rest of the night in my room, pretending to study and trying not to think about Duncan and Holiday sitting in the plush darkness of a theater across the river, whispering about what a philistine I was. Around nine I shuffled down to the convenience store, cobbling dinner together out of a microwave pizza, a bag of Pepperidge Farm Brussels cookies, and a waxy Red Delicious apple, for health.

"Dude," Dave said when I got back upstairs, eyeing me over his laptop. "You good?"

"I'm fine," I snapped, then winced at the sound of it. "Sorry." I scrubbed a hand over my face. "Just, like, a lot on my mind."

Dave nodded. "They're doing an overnight Indiana Jones marathon in the common room," he offered. "I'm going to go by when I'm done with this paper, if you want to come along."

I shook my head. "I think I might just crash," I said, partly because I wanted to see what time Duncan got home and partly because I had, by this point, eaten thirteen of the fifteen cookies in the foil-lined Pepperidge Farm bag and was feeling more than a little bit ill. "But thanks."

Dave shrugged. "Suit yourself," he said, shutting his computer and heaving himself up off the bed. "You change your mind about whatever you're sulking over, you know where to find me."

"I'm not *sulking*," I said peevishly. And I wasn't.

Not exactly.

Okay, I was sulking a little.

Holiday was just wrong, that was all. She had no idea what she was talking about. It wasn't true; I did so ask her questions. And if I didn't, it was only because she was always talking so much that

I could barely get a word in edgewise. Still, when I tried to make a list of things I knew about her life right now, it was disturbingly short.

Ugh, I really did not want to be the bad guy here.

Fight with Holiday or not, the end of the semester was speeding in my direction like a car down the turnpike, assignments stacking up one on top of another. I was painstakingly formatting the bibliography for an expos paper I was writing on women historians of the IRA the following afternoon when my phone buzzed on the table beside me. *How's the work going?* Greer wanted to know.

Miserable, I reported. *What's up?*

Look out your window.

I leaned back in my chair and peered down at the outside of Hemlock House, where Greer was standing in her bright red pea-coat and a hat with a pompom on it, her hair glossy and dark. I watched as she waved, then bent her head to type something else into her phone: *Study break?* she asked.

I grinned, slamming my laptop closed and pushing my chair back. *Sure.*

I grabbed my coat, thundering down the stairs and out into the courtyard, which was bustling with all the frenetic activity of a Friday afternoon. "I know you," I said, wrapping my arms around Greer in the chilly afternoon light. We hadn't seen a ton of each other since we'd gotten back from Maine; I'd been distracted by my goose chase after Margot, and she'd been gearing up for the final push of the semester. "I figured you were in the library."

"I was," she said, "but my brain is soup." She wrinkled her nose. "You wanna go have an adventure?"

We took the train across the river and got off the Green Line at the Prudential Center, the high-end mall already decked out for the holidays in reds and golds. "Are we going to Eataly?" I asked hopefully.

Greer laughed. "Maybe later," she promised, pulling me through the crowd of shoppers and out onto Huntington Ave. "If you're good."

Outside the mall it was freezing; I'd forgotten this about Boston in winter, how the wind comes in off the water and slices through the buildings, burning your face and the inside of your ears. The Berkshires were cold, sure, but not like this. "I'm transferring," I decided. "Effective immediately. And I'm only applying to schools in Florida."

Greer ignored me, pulling me through the afternoon crowds on the sidewalk before finally coming to a stop in front of an empty reflecting pool, which stretched out in front of us for the better part of a block. A few skateboarders in skullcaps practiced their moves, wheels rumbling over the concrete. "Here we are," she announced. "I've always wanted to come to this place."

"Oh yeah?" I teased. "Hoping to get some tips on your ollies?"

"You're hilarious." She shook her head. "Not the pool," she said, then motioned at the hulking building at the other side of the reflecting pool. "The Mapparium."

I shook my head. "The what, now?"

"Come on," Greer said, then took my hand and pulled me toward the entrance.

The Mapparium was an enormous, inside-out stained-glass globe lit up with a million tiny light bulbs. "Whoa," I said as we stepped onto the long glass walkway that cut down the middle—startling at how loud and booming my voice sounded, gazing around at the world with no small amount of wonder. There was something strange happening with the perspective from this angle, the sizes of the continents all different from what I was used to seeing: Africa way bigger than it looked on the globe in my bedroom back at my mom's house; Europe and North America huddled as if for warmth right up against the North Pole. "This is wild."

"It's cool, right?" Greer asked, turning a slow circle on the catwalk with her hands tucked into her pockets. Her tone was nonchalant, careless even, but I could see in the eager lift of her eyebrows that she was hoping I'd say yes.

"It's really cool," I agreed softly. Cooler still was the idea that she'd brought me here hoping I'd like it, that she'd picked it out for a field trip with me in mind. All at once I felt a wave of fondness for her that was so strong it almost took me out at the knees. How had I spent almost two years apart from her? How had I forgotten the way she made me feel? "I can't believe I didn't know it was here."

Greer's eyes were shining. "It gets cooler," she told me, motioning along the walkway back the way we'd come. "Here, go stand at that end."

I did as she told me, watching as she made her way to the opposite side of the globe. "Hi," she whispered—or at least, I could tell by the way her mouth was moving that it was a whisper. The acoustics of the Mapparium made it so I could hear her as loudly and clearly as if she'd been speaking right into my ear.

"It's a whispering gallery," she told me, her smile radiant on the other side of the world. "It's for telling secrets."

"Oh yeah?" I felt the back of my neck get warm. "Tell me one, then, how about."

Greer tapped a finger to her lips, like she was thinking. "I'm really glad you came to Harvard," she confessed after a moment. "I think maybe I've been letting you feel like I didn't care so much one way or the other. I think maybe I wanted you to believe that, even. But I'm really happy you're here."

"I'm really happy I am too." I grinned at her, the warmth in my chest enough to power the entire planet. I could feel the weirdness from my fight with Holiday—the heaviness I'd been carrying ever since Bri died—melting away. I looked at Greer standing there across the walkway, hands still tucked neatly into the pockets of her bright red coat. I loved her, I realized. And I was tired of sneaking around, keeping secrets and telling half-truths like the scared, insecure kid I'd been when we were together back at Bartley. I wanted to be honest with her. I wanted to be the kind of grown-ass man she deserved. "I have to tell you something," I said.

Greer laughed. "I mean," she replied, in her normal voice this time, "that's kind of the idea."

But I shook my head. "I'm serious."

Her smile slipped, just a little. "Okay," she agreed slowly, taking a cautious step toward me and tilting her head back toward the door. "Should we go?"

We grabbed lattes at a nearby Starbucks and sat on a bench outside the Mapparium, both of us shivering a little bit in the gray

New England afternoon. "Are you breaking up with me?" Greer asked, running her thumb in circles around the plastic lid of her coffee cup. "Because I gotta say, Linden, if you chased me around all semester just to dump me two weeks before finals—"

"I'm not," I promised quickly. "I'm definitely not."

"Okay," she said. "Then what?"

"First of all," I began, then cleared my throat and started over. "First of all, please believe me when I say I know this is going to sound completely bonkers. And also, I know you're probably going to be pissed."

"Oh, boy." Greer looked at me sidelong. "Gotta love a conversation that starts that way."

"Yeah." I took a deep breath. "So, um, here's the thing. I know Margot and James are hooking up. And I know that you know too, but I think the thing you might *not* know is that they *know* you know, and that's why they tried to hurt you, but wound up accidentally getting Bri instead."

For a moment Greer just gaped at me, the only sounds the cars on Huntington Avenue and the frigid wind screaming across the plaza. It felt like the first moment after a gunshot. "To begin with," she said finally, her voice small in the sudden hugeness of the city all around us, "um, no. I definitely did not know that."

"Oh. Well." I felt myself blush, like possibly I was the pervert here. "Margot and James are hooking up."

"Margot and James are first cousins."

"I know," I said.

"And they're—"

"Yeah." I winced. "I saw it. I wish I could unsee it, actually."

Greer didn't laugh. "Where?" she asked. "Like, when did you—how do you even know that?"

"It doesn't matter."

"Were you spying on them?" She stood up so fast her coffee burbled up like a geyser, flooding the lid of her cup. "Have you been spying on *me*?"

"Of course not," I said, scrambling to my feet to match her. "Why would I spy on you?" I shook my head. "I just—it started because when we were at Margot's at Thanksgiving I saw this text on her phone—"

"You were going through her *phone*?"

"She handed it to me!" I protested. "The text popped up while I was taking that video of you guys doing the dance from *High School Musical* or whatever."

"First of all, it was *A Goofy Movie*," Greer corrected me. "And second of all, you realize how sketchy you sound right now."

"I do, yes." I sighed, setting my coffee cup down on the bench. "Anyway, the point is—"

"The *point* is," Greer interrupted, "this is ridiculous. Even if it is true about Margot and James—and I will tell you right now, I think that is a *big* if—Margot was with me in the library the night Bri died, Linden. She felt bad for me about missing the lax party, so she came and brought me snacks and was generally a really good fucking friend to me, right up until the moment that we left Widener together and she dropped me off outside your dorm. There's no way she went up to the suite and killed Bri, thinking it was me: she knew I wasn't in there. On top of which, she's my friend, and she wouldn't try to hurt me. And if she *did* try to hurt me for some wild, enormously unlikely reason, she wouldn't have accidentally hurt Bri instead." Greer shook her head before I could say anything. "Look, Linden. I care about you. I love you, even—or I could, if you'd relax and give me a chance. But you have *got* to stop this. It's too much for me. It's freaking me out. It's making me worry about you."

I frowned. "Worry about me?"

Greer shrugged, sitting back down on the bench and wrapping her hands around her coffee cup. "I've seen what this school does to people who aren't ready for it," she said. "It makes you weird. It makes you a little impulsive. Before you know it you're fixating on shit that doesn't matter, just to feel like there's some part of your life that you can control." She lifted an eyebrow behind her glasses. "Believe me, I know. At this rate, you're going to wind up on academic probation, freaking out before every little quiz because you're terrified this is going to be the one that gets you booted, fooling around with your high school boyfriend."

I snorted, the tension draining out of my body as I reached for her, pulling her up again and into my arms. "There are worse things than fooling around with your high school boyfriend," I reminded her quietly.

Greer sighed. "Yes," she agreed with theatrical resignation, looping her arms around my neck. "I suppose there are."

We stood there for a long moment and held on to each other, cold wind buffeting us from all sides. "Get a room!" a skateboarder called from the other side of the plaza. I huffed a laugh into Greer's hair.

"Okay," I decided finally. "You're right. I'm sorry. I'm going to stop. I am stopping; I have officially stopped. I'm done playing Sherlock Holmes. I just want to get through my finals and finish the rest of the semester and be with you."

"Sounds like a plan," Greer agreed, her voice muffled into my jacket. She pulled back to look at me then, her eyes searching my face behind her glasses like she wanted to make sure I wasn't full of shit. "I want this to work, Linden. I, like—really, *really* want this to work."

I thought of the first time I'd ever seen her, in the library back at Bartley. I thought of how it felt to run into her that day in the Coop. "Me too," I promised. "And I'm sorry."

Greer nodded. "Buy me dinner to make it up to me, how about?"

I grinned. "You got a deal."

19

WE WENT TO DINNER AT A PLACE GREER LIKED IN Chinatown, tucking ourselves into a tiny table by the fogged-up window and ordering a mess of steamed buns and udon noodles. "What are you doing for the break?" Greer asked over the clank of dishes from the kitchen.

Trying to find odd jobs and avoiding Holiday, probably, but I didn't say that out loud. "Still considering my options," I told her instead, hooking an ankle around hers underneath the wobbly table. "Why, are you traveling?"

Greer nodded. "I think Vail, maybe?" She heaped a pile of noodles onto her plate. "We'll see what happens when grades come back, though. It's possible my dad will make me stay in Connecticut practicing Latin conjugation to atone for my unextraordinary mind."

"I think you're pretty extraordinary," I told her, no hesitation. Greer flicked a piece of green onion at my head.

We got an Uber back to campus. It was freezing, the wind

damp and that bite in the air that tempts snow; Greer slipped her hand into mine as we crossed the courtyard toward Hemlock House, tugging me close like we could keep each other warm that way. "You could come with me," she murmured. "Over break, I mean."

I looked down at her as we made our way through the lobby, interested. "To Vail, you mean?"

Greer grinned. "Or to Connecticut," she said with a shrug. "I might need some help with my irregular verbs."

We swung by the suite to pick up a bottle of wine Greer had squirreled away in her closet, then climbed the stairs to my empty room. Both of us had work to do, so Greer put on a jazzy, Starbucks-y playlist she said would help us focus, the two of us sitting side by side in my bed clacking away at our computers. Duncan and Dave got back from the library around midnight, bearing fries and shakes from Tasty Burger. All of us were asleep by one a.m.

I woke up the following morning to a knock on the door. The light was gray and blurry out the window when I cracked one eye open; I was confused for a second, thinking I was back at home in Eastie and my mom was knocking to tell me that school had been canceled for snow. Then I blinked and remembered.

"What the fuck," Dave mumbled, rooting around for his glasses as whoever it was knocked again, louder and more insistently this time. "What time is it?"

"Early." I climbed over Greer, who was only just stirring, and padded barefoot across the carpet to swing the door open. "Yeah?"

"Michael Linden?"

I blinked. Standing silhouetted against the harsh light of the hallway were the same two campus security guards Holiday had shaken down to let us look at the entry log for Hemlock House. "Um," I said, a second of keen white fear slicing through me that something terrible had happened to my mom while I was across the river drinking goldfish and reading Derrida like an asshole. "Yes? That's me."

"We've had a report of stolen property in this room," said the taller one—DiNapoli, I remembered. I wasn't sure if I was imagining the look of gleeful satisfaction on his face. "We'd like to conduct a search."

I didn't answer for a moment, my brain sluggish with sleep and confusion. "A search?" I repeated slowly, trying to figure out what the fuck I should do here. I knew Holiday would tell them to come back with a warrant—but did campus security even need a warrant to search a dorm? I didn't know, on top of which I was in my heart, and had always been, a rule follower. Also: I had nothing to hide. "Yeah, okay." I looked at Duncan and Dave, who were both sitting up dazedly in their bunk beds. "I mean, if it's okay with you guys?"

They nodded in unison.

"Um, what's this about?" Greer asked, swinging her legs over the side of the bed and reaching for her tortoiseshell glasses, her brow furrowed as she slipped them onto her face. "I mean, what are you looking for, exactly?" She turned to me. "Do you know what they're looking for?"

"I have no idea," I promised quickly, swallowing down the reflexive kind of guilt you feel when people are accusing you of something, even when you know objectively you haven't done anything wrong. I watched as the two of them opened my drawers and pawed through my closet—with, frankly, a lot less elegance and finesse than Holiday and I had when we'd been going through Hunter's stuff back at the lax house. "Who was the report from?"

"That's not information we're able to share," the shorter one said—or started to, anyway. He was interrupted by a quiet sound of satisfaction from his partner:

"Welp," DiNapoli announced, his beefy hands buried in my underwear drawer, "here we go."

I looked over, my mouth falling slightly open in abject shock: there was Greer's watch—the vintage Rolex, big and heavy and elegant—gleaming quietly in the morning light.

I gasped, I couldn't help it. Duncan and Dave looked on in horror. Greer stared at me for a moment, a thousand different expressions flickering across her face. "Linden," she said finally, and her voice was almost preternaturally calm. "What the *fuck* are you doing with my grandpa's watch?"

"Greer," I said, gaping back at her. "I have no idea. I have no fucking idea! Somebody planted it in there. Somebody's setting me up. Come on, you've gotta know somebody's setting me up." It sounded ridiculous. It *was* ridiculous, like something out of a campy film noir. "Greer," I said again. "Come on."

But Greer wasn't listening. "Can I have it back?" she asked the security guards. Her voice was very small. "My watch, I mean."

The shorter one shook his head. "We need to photograph and log it as evidence first—"

"Evidence?" I was almost shouting. "It's not *evidence* of anything."

"—but you can file a claim with the university, and it'll be returned to you once the disciplinary hearings are done."

Greer nodded. "Okay," she said, rubbing a hand over her face. She looked exhausted, the hollows under her eyes bluish in the pale light of morning. "Thank you."

My heart was racing. "Greer—"

"Don't, Linden." She barely spared me a glance before turning back to the guards. "Can I go, then? Like, do you need me to . . ." She trailed off, waving a hand in a way that presumably meant *act as a witness for Linden's summary execution.*

"Sure," one of them said, looking to his partner for confirmation. "I don't see why not."

"Great," she said. "I guess I will . . . do that, then." She turned back to Dave and Duncan. "I'll see you guys around, I guess? I don't even—"

"Greer!" I tried again, and this time she whirled on me.

"I don't know what's going on," she said, "and honestly, I don't really want to know. But you've been acting weird ever since we started hanging out again. And I've been trying to tell myself it's fine, that it doesn't matter, that I'm just grateful to have you back in my life, but now—like, is that why you wanted to get back together? So you could *steal* from me?" She shook her head. "Did you hurt Bri too?"

"Of course not," I said, momentarily dizzy. "Stop."

"We're going to need you to come with us to the dean's office," DiNapoli announced, putting a hand on my arm. I resisted the urge to jerk away, but barely. I felt like I was floating somewhere up near the ceiling, watching this whole thing happen to someone else.

"I've gotta get out of here," Greer said, so quietly it might have only been to herself. "I've gotta go." She grabbed her phone off the nightstand and brushed past the security guards, the swish of her hair the last thing I saw before I turned around to face whatever was about to happen next.

20

Saturday, 12/14/24

THE SKY WAS JUST TURNING FROM BLACK TO GRAY outside the window of my bedroom when my mom knocked on the door, light from the hallway spilling across the carpet. "I'm heading out," she said softly, "but I left the coffee on."

"Thanks," I managed, blinking into the sleep-stale dimness. "What time is it?"

"It's early," she said. "The mutual aid group is handing out coffee and doughnuts at Mass and Cass, but I should be back by lunchtime." She paused. "You going to be all right?"

"I'm fine," I lied, trying to muster my most convincing smile. I was seven days into a ten-day administrative suspension, due back on campus right in time for finals—assuming, of course, that I was ultimately cleared of any wrongdoing, which wasn't at all a sure thing. Greer wasn't answering any of my texts. *Nobody* was answering any of my texts, actually, with the exception of Coach Lyons, who'd written a terse email letting me know that my involvement on the team next semester was contingent upon the findings of the

Disciplinary Board. "My entire life is contingent upon the findings of the Disciplinary Board," I'd muttered uselessly, then sent the message to the trash without bothering to reply.

"Okay," my mom said now, hovering in the doorway a moment longer. She was plucky, but I could tell she felt outmatched by the accusations against me, by the hugeness of the Harvard machine. I couldn't blame her—I felt outmatched by it too. "Eat something, will you? There are some corn muffins left from yesterday, whenever you get up."

"I will," I promised. "Have fun."

Once she was gone I rolled over and stared at the wall for a while, which was the same way I'd spent most of the week since I'd gotten kicked out of housing. I dozed for a little bit longer. I sulked. I imagined alternate lives for myself: I could go back to working at Market Basket, I thought, where I'd been a checker for a couple of summers. I could coach peewee lacrosse, although actually probably not if I had a criminal record. I could light out for the open West like Jack Kerouac, though I wasn't entirely sure how I'd pay for gas or what I'd do once I got there. I was pretty sure Market Basket was only a Massachusetts thing.

I was reaching for my phone to Google *California grocery store chains* when the buzzer rang. "Hello?" I asked, shuffling down the hallway with my blanket around my shoulders like a cape and pressing the button on the intercom.

"I have a confession," Holiday announced, her voice crackling through the ancient speaker. "I drove down Cambridge Street the other day. And the *Live Poultry Fresh Killed* sign is in fact gone."

"It is?" I asked—startled, trying to ignore the weird thing my heart did at the sound of her voice. We hadn't talked since our fight on the T platform, though I knew she'd probably heard from Duncan about what had happened with the campus police. "I'm surprised, actually. My money would have been on you."

"I mean, that's because I'm usually right," she admitted. "But, you know. Not always."

"Most of the time," I said quietly, and hit the button to let her upstairs.

❧

"I owe you an apology," I told her when I opened the door a minute later. She was wearing a parka the size of a sleeping bag, her dark hair in an enormous knot on top of her head.

"You do," she agreed immediately. "But I'm not here for that."

"You're not?" I raised my eyebrows, my gaze even on hers. "What are you here for?"

Holiday cleared her throat. "I'll tell you in the car," she said, stepping past me into the apartment. "Go get dressed."

"Where are we going?"

"Field trip," she told me, her dark eyes shining. "And we're kind of on a schedule here, so, you know." She nodded in the direction of my bedroom. "Pitter patter."

For the first time in a week I felt myself lighten, something rusted shut inside me creaking open a fraction of an inch. Biggest fight of our entire relationship or not, if Holiday was here, that meant everything wasn't over yet. Endless weirdness between us notwithstanding, she had still shown up.

"Okay," I said, and headed for the hallway. At the last second I turned and grabbed her arm, pulling her around to face me; I overshot, though, and we wound up nose to nose. "Um," she said as I let go in a hurry. "Hi."

"Hi." I took a deep breath. "I'm really sorry I didn't come to your showcase," I told her. "I should have—" I broke off, holding my hands up a little helplessly. "I should have."

Holiday tilted her head. "I mean," she said calmly. "Yes."

"You're my best friend," I continued. "You've *always* been my best friend, even when we weren't talking, ever since the time we were four and I shoved my hand up the bathtub faucet at your parents' house and it got caught."

"I did save your ass that day," Holiday mused, the hint of a smile quirking at the very edges of her mouth. "If it wasn't for me you'd probably still be sitting there alone, crying."

"I'd definitely be sitting *somewhere* alone and crying," I agreed. "I get stuck up my own ass sometimes, you know that. *I* know that. But I can do a better job. I *want* to do a better job."

Holiday seemed to think about that for a moment. "My room-mate's name is Ebony," she said finally, "and she's great."

"I'm glad," I told her, and I meant it. "You deserve great people in your life. Which brings me to my next point, which is that I was being a dick about Duncan for no reason. Obviously if you guys want to—I mean, not that you need my—" I shook my head. "You know what I mean." I sighed. "I'm really sorry, Holiday."

Holiday nodded, holding my gaze for a moment; for a second it seemed like she might be about to tell me something, but in the end she just jerked one thumb at the door. "Put your clothes on," she said finally, "and let's go."

21

Saturday, 12/14/24

"YOU KNOW," I SAID FORTY MINUTES LATER, SITTING IN the passenger seat of Holiday's filthy car as we cruised through Newton, a tony suburb west of Boston, "clearly I am not in a position to be questioning anything about your investigative methods at this particular moment. But one *might* make the argument that I'd be a more effective stakeout partner if you'd tell me what we're looking for."

"Who says we're even on a stakeout?" Holiday shot back, flicking on her turn signal with a flourish. "I mean, for all you know I'm just taking the scenic route back to my dorm. There's something I need on a high shelf that I can't reach."

"You're taller than I am," I pointed out.

Holiday's smile was brilliant. "I know."

She turned left, then right again—navigating without the benefit of her phone or any map that I could locate, like possibly she had the entire road atlas of the Commonwealth of Massachusetts tucked neatly away in her brain—before finally pulling into the parking lot of the public high school and cruising to a stop in front of the main entrance. "Okay," I said as she pulled the parking brake. "Now what?"

But Holiday only shrugged. "I don't know, Michael. You did miss my stage debut," she reminded me. "I feel like I'm entitled to a few theatrics." She nodded at the entrance, where a steady trickle of high schoolers were making their way through the main entrance, heads ducked against the sharp December wind. "SATs today," she observed.

"Thinking of reapplying?" I teased. "Going to try to get into business school after all?"

Holiday shook her head. "They couldn't handle me."

"That's a fact."

We were silent for a moment, both of us watching the entrance. Harvard didn't require the SATs anymore—most schools didn't—but I'd taken them anyway, and so had most of my friends at Bartley. If you tanked, there was no obligation to submit the results to colleges. And if you did well, at the very least they knew you could take a test.

"How was it?" I asked finally, glancing at her sidelong. "Your showcase, I mean."

Holiday looked at me for a long time. "I nailed it," she said.

"Yeah," I said, a confusing mix of emotions surging through me—pride, regret, a weird chasm of longing. "Sounds about right." I took a deep breath. "Look, Holiday—"

But Holiday held up a hand to stop me. "*You* look," she said, pointing through the windshield. "Right there."

I squinted, following her gaze across the small plaza to where a blond in jeans and a nondescript gray hoodie was heading into the testing site. "Is that . . . Greer's cousin Emily?" I asked. "I don't— She goes to BU. What's she doing taking the SATs?"

"She doesn't go to BU," Holiday announced. "Her name isn't Emily. And she's not Greer's cousin."

I blinked. "Wait," I said as the girl—Not-Emily, apparently—disappeared inside. "What? Hang on a sec."

"Greer is on academic probation, right?" Holiday asked, sitting back in the driver's seat and pulling one leg up underneath her. "And when I was looking at your Bartley yearbooks when I was at your house that day, I didn't see her in any of the honor society pictures. It just made me wonder, you know—if she didn't have the grades to get into Harvard, and she wasn't like, a sports person or a computer prodigy or whatever, how did she wind up there?"

"Legacy," I said immediately. "Which is cringey, I know, but—"

"Would she have taken the chance on legacy, though? Like from what you said about the pressure she was under, would she have risked it?" Holiday lifted her chin in the direction of the entrance. "Or did she have an insurance policy?"

I shook my head, feeling defensive on Greer's behalf in spite of myself. "I don't know what that means."

Holiday blew a breath out. "That girl's real name is Corinne Hayes," she informed me. "She's an MIT dropout who works at the Apple Store in the South Shore mall, but she's *also,* as it turns out, got a nice little side hustle taking the SATs for would-be Ivy Leaguers who aren't sure they can get the job done on their own."

"But Emily—"

"There *is* no Emily, Michael."

"Wait wait wait." I blinked. "Like, at all?"

Holiday shook her head. "At least, not that I could find. And trust me: I *looked.*"

"I know you did," I said slowly. "I know."

"Did Greer ever mention a cousin before that day at the football game?"

I thought about that for a moment, racking my memory. "No," I admitted finally. "I guess she didn't."

"It took me a long time, but the other night I finally figured out where I recognized her from," Holiday told me. "Corinne, I mean. She was on the security camera footage when we were looking for Hunter. She went into Hemlock a couple of minutes before he did." Her lips twisted. "You might have noticed her too, if you hadn't been so busy arguing with the security guard over the technicalities of goldfish swallowing."

I rubbed a hand over my face, trying to put the pieces together. "So Greer hired this girl Corinne to take the SATs for her. And then—" I thought of the note underneath the bed: *you owe me.* I thought of seeing Corinne leaving Hemlock the day Greer's room got tossed. "Our theory is what, exactly? Corinne came after Greer for money? But got Bri instead?"

"Yes," Holiday said, "and no."

"Is that all you're going to tell me?"

She shrugged. "Michael," she said, and her voice was so quiet. "Let me be a little bit impressive right now, will you?"

I opened my mouth, closed it again. "Sure," I said. "Of course."

Holiday nodded briskly at that, putting the car in drive and glancing over her shoulder as she pulled out of the parking lot. "Buckle up, partner," she instructed, her dark eyes shining. "We're going back to school."

22

Saturday, 12/14/24

IT FELT LIKE A LOT LONGER THAN A WEEK SINCE I'D
been on campus. I looked around uneasily as we climbed the steps
of Hemlock House, feeling like Rip Van Winkle waking up after
a hundred years. "You ready?" Holiday asked as we made our way
down the hall. I couldn't quite get myself to reply.

It was Greer who opened the door of the suite. "What are you
doing here?" she asked, her dark gaze darting back and forth between Holiday and me. "Did they clear you?"

"Not yet, actually," I admitted a little sheepishly. On the ride
over here I'd been happy to take Holiday's lead, but all at once I
wished I'd made her tell me exactly what we were doing here: how
to play this, what to say. "Li-Wen let us up. Can we come in?"

"I don't know if that's a good idea." That was Dagny, with
Keiko and Margot close behind her and Celine bringing up the
rear; they clustered behind Greer in the doorway, a quartet of
Chanel-scented bodyguards.

Holiday cleared her throat. "Hi," she said, holding a hand up and smiling her sanest smile. "I don't know if you all remember me. We met at the football game; I'm Holiday, I'm Linden's friend. I know it's a Saturday, and that you guys must be busy with finals, on top of which you've all obviously been through, like, a ton of shit this semester. This will only take a second."

"What will?" Keiko asked, but Holiday was already slipping neatly past her into the common room, perching on the arm of the sofa.

"I just was hoping to talk to Greer really quick," she said, like it was the most reasonable thing in the world. "About the night Bri died."

"Oh, my god, when are you guys going to drop this!" Greer whirled on us. "I'm not doing this with you. I'm not."

Dagny frowned. "Greer—"

"They think somebody was trying to kill me and got Bri instead," Greer announced, "which is delusional, clearly. And they're been like, snooping around trying to prove it, or at least that's what they said they were doing—"

"Holy shit," Dagny said. "Why didn't you say anything?"

"Because it's embarrassing!" Greer exploded. "And it's weird! And it's frankly fucking scary, so—"

"You guys are guests here," Margot interrupted, turning to me and to Holiday. "You don't even *go* to Harvard, and I don't even think you're technically allowed on campus right now, Linden, so I don't know what you think you're doing just like barging in here and—"

"Making wild accusations?" Holiday supplied. "No, totally. I agree. And I owe you an apology, Greer, because we were wrong to think somebody was coming after you. That's not actually what happened at all."

"Okay," Margot said, holding her hands up. "This is silly. I'm going to go get the RA—"

"You told Linden you were in the library with Margot until it closed the night that Bri died," Holiday said to Greer, "which as far as I can tell is probably true. But what you didn't mention is that Margot peeled off afterward—to go to BU, if I had to guess—"

Keiko's eyes narrowed quizzically. "Why BU?" she asked Margot, but Holiday was still talking.

"—while you came back to Hemlock before you went to Linden's room. And you had someone with you: Corinne Hayes." She turned to look at me, anticipating my question. "The two of them were together, on the camera footage. I didn't want to say anything because—" She broke off, but I knew why. A couple of years ago Holiday had posited someone I cared about as a suspect, and it had almost been the end of our friendship. There was no way she'd have said anything this time unless she was absolutely sure.

"Wait a second," Dagny said. "Who the fuck is Corinne Hayes?"

"That's a great question," Holiday said. "Corinne Hayes took the SATs for Greer. Did she write your essays too?" she asked, turning to look at her. "I know she does essays, but they're expensive."

"You have no idea what you're talking about," Greer snapped.

"She was shaking you down, right?" Holiday sounded almost sympathetic. "Escalating. Leaving creepy notes where your suitemates might find them. Trashing your room. Threatening to rat you out to your parents—or worse—if you didn't keep paying, which is why you started stealing things—including, I'm pretty sure, your own watch. A nice touch, by the way. Very clever to throw suspicion off yourself right from the get-go. I would have done the same thing.

"My guess is that she came back for more the night of the party at the lax house," Holiday continued—she was enjoying herself now, I could see it, her posture relaxing as she perched on the arm of the couch. "And what were you going to do? You were in it now. You'd done it. It was way too late. You couldn't risk anybody seeing you give her the money out in the open, so you brought her up here thinking the suite would be empty. Bri must have come back from the party, heard you guys arguing, and freaked out. You couldn't pay her off too, probably. She was drunk, she was high. She was going to out you. You fought. And it got out of hand." She turned to me. "We were wrong from the very beginning, Linden. It was never a case of mistaken identity. Nobody was ever after Greer. Greer killed Bri to keep her secret."

I felt myself get light-headed, the blood draining from my skull. I don't know what I'd been expecting, but it wasn't this. "Holiday," I started, but Celine cut me off.

"This is ridiculous," she announced, pulling Greer behind her like Greer was a child and we were a couple of perverts lurking on the playground. "Like, what in the actual fuck is happening right now? Who the fuck do you think you are? We all know you're here on scholarship, Linden. We all know you never have any cash. So if this is some messed-up way to try to shift the blame off you for stealing shit from people who trusted you, then—"

"Don't," Greer interrupted. "Celine, come on, don't say that."

"Are you serious?" Dagny whirled on her. "Why are you

defending him right now? We're your friends, Greer. We're not about to sit here and let him use what happened to Bri as some excuse to call you a fucking *murderer*—"

"That's not what we're saying," I interrupted reflexively.

"It's exactly what you're saying!" Margot looked at me like I was deranged. "It is literally exactly what you guys just said. Like, does that make you feel good about yourself, to waltz in here and say that shit to a person who's grieving—"

"Stop," Greer said, holding a hand up. "All of you, just—"

"You stop, Greer! I'm not going to let them come into our house and say you killed our fucking suitemate in cold blood. Like, did you kill our suitemate in cold blood? Of course not, so—"

"It wasn't like that," Greer said quietly. "That's not what it was like."

Just for one second, none of us breathed. "Greer," I murmured, and I swore I could feel my heart breaking deep inside my chest. "Oh, Greer."

"It *wasn't*," she insisted, shaking her head a little. "Bri was my best friend. I loved her. The same way I love all of you." She slid down the wall into a crouch, wrapping her arms around her knees like she wanted to make herself as small as humanly possible. "But she was just so *outraged*, you know? It was like she didn't even know me, like she was just going on and on about fairness and integrity, like she had any kind of leg to stand on. That whole *I'm just the humble daughter of a car salesman* thing that she liked to do? Her dad literally plays golf with the dean of admissions on Nantucket every summer. It's not like she got here through brains and grit. But she just looked so disappointed in me, you know? It made me feel insane. And she was going on and on and she was just so *noisy.*" She turned to the girls. "You guys know how she was. A voice like a fucking foghorn. Even on a Saturday with nobody around, somebody was going to hear. I didn't mean to hurt her. I just needed her to stop yelling before someone heard.

"You guys don't know what it was like," she continued. "Not coming here was never an option. My grades weren't great. I'm not a violin prodigy or a field hockey star. I'm just . . . average. I always have been. And there is absolutely nothing my parents hate more than that."

It was Margot, in the end, who found her voice first. "Greer, sweetheart," she said. She sounded so kind. "We have to tell someone."

Greer looked at her for a moment. "I know," she said quietly, and started to cry.

Margot hugged her then. The other three joined them, the five of them holding each other, connected in their grief and their love for each other. They looked like a Renaissance painting, like something you'd see hanging in the Isabella Stewart Gardner Museum across town. It felt like we were intruding.

"Come on," Holiday said, putting a gentle hand on my arm and nodding toward the exit.

"What?" I murmured, surprised. I was waiting on the grand finale; I figured she'd have somehow texted a buddy on the Cambridge Police Department on the way over here, or sent out a distress signal via the 311 app. "Don't we need to make sure—?"

"No," Holiday said, "we don't." She shook her head. "They can handle it from here."

23

Afterward

HOLIDAY WAS RIGHT ABOUT THAT TOO, IN THE END. THE girls from the suite went with Greer to the dean of students; from there, they went with her to turn herself in to the police. The story made the front page of every paper in town, from the *Globe* to the *Crimson;* I turned my face away from the headlines as I trudged across campus to hand in my final paper for International Women Writers. Technically, I could have just uploaded it to the portal—I was probably going to have to upload it to the portal anyhow, actually—but I'd never managed to make it to my mandatory advisor meeting and figured this was probably my last chance.

"Michael," Professor McMorrow said, lifting one eyebrow when I knocked on the open door to her office. It was winter gray outside the window, a glass-shaded lamp casting a warm glow across the desk. "Nice to see you back."

"Nice to be back," I said, handing over the paper. "Was a little touch and go there for a minute."

The professor nodded like *No kidding.* "How was your first semester?"

"Eventful."

She leaned back in her leather chair. "I can imagine."

I tucked my hands into my coat pockets, clearing my throat a bit. Her office was cozy, the walls lined with novels and collections of poetry, classical music piping from a little Bose radio on the shelf. On the desk was a framed photograph of the professor on the beach with a woman I assumed was her wife, each of them holding a squirmy-looking toddler. "I owe you an apology," I told her. "I was . . . amped, the last time we talked."

McMorrow raised an eyebrow. "That's one word for it, certainly."

"I was an inappropriate jerk," I clarified, "and I'm sorry."

She waved her hand. "I've seen worse. And knowing what we know now, I imagine you were going through quite a bit in your personal life."

"You could say that," I agreed. "I'm hoping the rest of my time here isn't quite so high-stakes. Or like, that it *is* high-stakes, but maybe not in quite the same way as this was?" I was rambling, the wildness of the last days and weeks catching up with me all at once. "I've been thinking a lot about what I'm trying to get from my time here, is I guess what I'm saying."

"And?" She lifted her chin.

"A friend of mine told me I should be sure not to waste it."

"Sounds like good advice."

"Yeah," I agreed. "She's . . . smart like that. Anyway, I think I'm ready to declare a major."

That seemed to surprise her. "You've got time, you know," she reminded me. "I don't know if I was quite obvious the last time we spoke. There's no requirement to declare until November of your sophomore year."

"No, I know," I assured her, "but I want to. It feels really obvious to me now, what I want to study here. It feels really clear to me what I want to do."

McMorrow nodded one more time, then reached over to turn down the music before gesturing to the empty chair on the other side of her desk. "Well, in that case," she said, "have a seat, why don't you? You can tell me a little bit more about what you have in mind."

༺༻

I told Holiday a few nights later as we walked through Cambridge Common, steam from her cup of hot chocolate curling up around her face. "Psychology," she repeated, her smile glowing. "Of course. I love it. I think it's perfect."

"I mean, I don't know about *perfect,*" I said, feeling the back of my neck prickle under the collar of my jacket. They'd lit the big tree a few weeks before, the bulbs glowing cheerily in the twilight. "But I keep coming back to it, how what happened with Greer didn't come out of nowhere. And how what happened on the Vineyard didn't either." I shrugged, a little embarrassed. "Anyway, it's interesting to me, how brains work. Why people do the things that they do."

"Not to mention the fact that it's a pretty useful field of study for a person who wants to pursue investigative work."

I raised an eyebrow. "Not to mention that, no."

"You know," Holiday said, perching on the edge of a park bench and crossing her ankles, "if we're going to keep doing this, we're going to need to have business cards printed up or something."

"Get a website," I agreed wryly. Bri's murder had made national news, the keyboard warriors on Reddit calling Greer the Ivy League Killer. There was a part of me that couldn't help but wonder if her parents might finally be a tiny bit impressed: after all, it had taken brains to do what she'd done. It had taken planning. It wasn't the work of—what had she said to me that night in Chinatown? An *unextraordinary mind.* "Punch up our SEO."

"Exactly." Holiday's tone was light, but a moment later she nudged me in the shoulder. "Are you okay? It's gotta be kind of a lot to process."

"I mean, yeah," I said with a shrug. "Not for nothing, but my romantic track record is . . . not so great the last couple of years. Forget a psychology major. I need to start with like, Remedial Human Relationships."

"Introduction to Heterosexual Mating Rituals, with a concentration in knowing whether the girl you're hooking up with has committed any felonies lately?"

"Maybe there's an online section," I mused. "Something I could take during J-term."

Holiday smiled. "Mine's not super either, for what it's worth," she said consolingly. "My track record, I mean. To be clear, it's definitely not as bad as *yours,* but still."

That interested me. "Oh no?" I asked, trying not to sound too eager. "What happened with Duncan?"

"I don't know," Holiday said with a shrug. "I think in the end I was kind of a lot of woman for him."

I nodded. "Well," I said slowly, "in that case. Can I ask you something?"

Holiday lifted an eyebrow. "Always."

"You wanna do something New Year's Eve?"

Holiday looked at me for a moment in the glow of the streetlights, a slow, knowing grin spreading across her face. "Maybe," she allowed. "We'll see." She tapped her cup against mine in a goofy little toast before standing up and disappearing into the crowd toward the Christmas tree, snow dusting her hair and the shoulders of her coat. I took a deep breath, then followed.

ACKNOWLEDGMENTS

Thanks to Wendy Loggia—I feel so lucky that Linden and Holiday (and I!) have found such a cozy home with you. Thanks to Alison Romig, for your keen eye and organizational acumen. Thanks to Tamar Schwartz and Cathy Bobak; thanks to Liz Dresner for the cover. Thanks to Jillian Vandall for being extremely lovely in addition to being very good at your job.

Thanks to Josh Bank, Sara Shandler, and Viana Siniscalchi for sixteen hours on the phone and six hours in the room together. It is still so much fun to work with you people, even after all this time. Thanks to Les Morgenstein. Thanks to Elizabeth Bewley for literally everything. Thanks to Katie Colleran for answering all my pedantic questions about Harvard even though I told you in advance I was just going to make things up if what you said was inconvenient for me. Thanks to Robin Benway, Corey Ann Haydu, Emery Lord, Jennifer Matthieu, and Elissa Sussman for your true friendship.

Thanks to my family, especially my sister. Thanks to Annie and Charlie, the two best people I know. Thanks to Tom, always, always. Would you look at this! We're doing it.

IS THERE A KILLER ON THE VINEYARD?
READ THE BOOK
THAT STARTED IT ALL . . .

NEW YORK TIMES BESTSELLING AUTHOR
KATIE COTUGNO

LIAR'S BEACH

IT'S A CRUEL SUMMER

ABOUT THE AUTHOR

Katie Cotugno is the *New York Times* bestselling author of *Liar's Beach* and seven messy, complicated feminist YA love stories, as well as the adult novel *Birds of California*. She is also the coauthor, with Candace Bushnell, of *Rules for Being a Girl*. Her books have been honored by the Junior Library Guild, the Bank Street Children's Book Committee, and the Kentucky Association of School Librarians, among others, and translated into more than fifteen languages. Katie is a Pushcart Prize nominee whose work has appeared in the *Iowa Review,* the *Mississippi Review,* and *Argestes,* as well as many other literary magazines. She studied Writing, Literature, and Publishing at Emerson College and received her MFA in Fiction at Lesley University. She lives in Boston with her family.

KATIECOTUGNO.COM